MW00831331

SEALED WITH STRENGTH

A CHRISTIAN ROMANTIC SUSPENSE

LAURA SCOTT

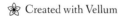

CHAPTER ONE

Sylvie McLane tugged her cowboy hat down on her head as she led her favorite mare, Fanny, along the north ridge of the McLane Mountain Ranch. After her father's cancer diagnosis, she'd taken over running the ranch, which had grown over the thirty-eight years her father had owned it. McLane Mountain was one of the most prosperous ranches in the area, and she was proud of what she and her dad had accomplished.

Now she needed to keep it going. No small feat in lean times of falling beef prices, not to mention the fact that most of the cowboys working for her chafed at taking orders from a woman. As if she hadn't learned anything in the past thirty-five years she'd lived and worked the ranch.

They'd just have to get over it. She preferred raising and training horses, but she wouldn't allow that to hold her back from taking over all aspects of the ranch. It was clear her younger brother, Sean, wasn't going to be much help.

"Whoa, girl," she murmured, tugging slightly on Fanny's reins to halt their progress. This spot offered the best view of the entire ranch, all fifteen hundred acres of it. The impressive sight never ceased to amaze her.

The gunshot came out of nowhere. Fanny shied, rising on her hind legs and pawing the air with her front hooves. Sylvie clenched her knees to stay seated, but Fanny turned so abruptly she felt herself losing her grip. Then Fanny rose again, throwing Sylvie off before bolting into the woods.

She hit the ground hard and rolled toward the edge of the ridge. Digging her hands into the earth, she tried to halt her momentum, but gravity pulled her toward the drop-off. She managed to find a tree root and clung to it with all the strength she possessed.

It was enough to stop her free fall. Yet her lower legs dangled over the edge. Using her toes, she tried to push against the cliff wall to lever herself up. It didn't work. If anything, she slipped another inch lower. Now more of her body was over the edge than not. The muscles in her arms quivered with exertion.

No! She couldn't die here today!

Sylvie swallowed hard and tried again to pull herself up. She was accustomed to physical labor, but she couldn't seem to get a good enough grip on the root. The flash of panic was impossible to ignore. How much longer could she hang here like a trout dangling from a line?

Not long.

Strong male hands clamped around one wrist, then the other. "I've got you."

Dawson Steele's face loomed over her, his features partially shadowed by the wide brim of his black cowboy hat. His blue eyes were full of concern as he held her. Normally, she'd be upset by his trespassing on her land. But when he began pulling her upright, she was keenly grateful for his strength.

Inch by inch, he pulled her up over the edge of the ridge. When she was mostly on solid ground, she was able to help by using her knees to scramble the rest of the way. Finally, Dawson let her go and rolled over onto his back, his hands pressing against his abdomen. A large, yellow lab with adorably floppy ears came over to sniff at him, then licked his face.

"Thank you." She frowned when Dawson seemed to be battling pain. "Hey, are you all right?"

"Yeah." The strain in his voice indicated otherwise. "Just need a minute."

She tried not to read too much into his comment, yet she knew she was sturdy and weighed a hundred and twenty-five pounds. No lightweight, that was for sure. Dawson had obviously hurt himself pulling her to safety. Maybe she needed to cut back on the carbs.

Finally, he pushed himself into a sitting position. He looped his arm around his dog, then glanced at her. "I had several abdominal surgeries over the past few months. The muscles are still tender, especially when I go overboard using them."

Abdominal surgeries, plural? "I'm sorry, I didn't know."

"How could you?" Dawson's tone held an edge. He stood and held out his hand to her. She accepted his help, trying to ignore the weird attraction she felt toward him. After twenty years of not seeing the guy while he served their country as a Navy SEAL, the past few months he'd popped in and out of her life several times.

It really annoyed her.

"Good thing that shooter didn't make his jack," Dawson drawled. She wanted to roll his eyes at his old western phrase of indicating the shooter had missed his mark. His tone was light, but his gaze was serious. "Any idea who set you in their sights?"

"I hope it wasn't you," she said tartly. "Why are you here anyway?"

He shook his head. "Still as prickly as ever, Sylvie. Why would I shoot you, then rush over to save your life? I was on Copper Creek property when I heard the gunfire. Saw you get busted off your horse, so I rode Diamond to get here as soon as I could. Thankfully, Kilo was able to keep up."

She glanced from his dog, Kilo, to Diamond, the gelding standing near a tree a few yards away. She flushed and nodded. It had been a long time since she'd been busted off a horse, that was for sure. "You're right, you did save my life. If you hadn't grabbed my arms . . ." She didn't finish the thought.

A shiver rippled down her spine as realization dawned slowly. Someone had just tried to kill her.

"I believe the gunfire came from the west," Dawson said. "Let's hop on Diamond and search for your horse."

"I might weigh too much for Diamond to carry us both," she protested.

"Don't be ridiculous. You're a lightweight." Dawson swung himself up into the saddle, a slight grimace creasing his features. Then he held out his hand.

She accepted his grip, then stepped up on his boot to swing herself up behind him. The saddle made riding together uncomfortable. She did her best to ignore being plastered up against Dawson. Hopefully, Fanny hadn't gone too far. The mare was known to be sure-footed, which is why she'd chosen her to ride the mountainside.

The gunfire had been close. Way too close. June wasn't hunting season, so it had to have been deliberate.

Who had taken the shot?

The why was obvious. Someone wanted to take the McLane Mountain Ranch now that her father was officially retired from ranching. Sylvie didn't want to believe her brother, Sean, had done this. Or her father's longtime ranch foreman, Josh O'Leary.

She wouldn't put it past her ex-husband, Paul Griffin, to try something like this. But she'd heard he'd moved to Boulder, Colorado.

"Sylvie? Is that your horse?" Dawson gestured to the wooded area up ahead.

She peered over Dawson's broad shoulder. "Yes, that's Fanny."

"Good-looking mare," he drawled.

"She's the best mountain trail horse I have." Normally, Fanny didn't startle easily, much less toss her rider. "The gunshot was too close and done purposely to spook her."

"Yeah, it was." He turned Diamond toward Fanny. The horses nickered a greeting to each other, making Sylvie smile despite her near-fatal fall from the cliff. "Any idea who would want you to eat dirt?"

"Unfortunately, there are several possibilities." She slid off Diamond's back. "Thanks again, Dawson."

"I'll escort you back to the ranch house."

She bent down to pat Kilo, then went over to grab Fanny's reins. She took a moment to physically examine the mare, making sure the animal wasn't hurt in any way. There were no obvious signs of injury, so she vaulted into the saddle and turned the mare toward Dawson. "I'm not going back, I need to ride the property. Thanks again."

"Hold on, Sylvie," Dawson protested. "You can't just pretend someone didn't take a shot at you."

"I'm not going to let that person prevent me from doing what's necessary." She was irritated with Dawson, partially because deep down she wanted nothing more than to head back to the ranch as he'd suggested. Every muscle in her body ached from the fall, and the idea of a long, hot bath tempted her beyond reason.

"Why not use your chopper to patrol the property?" Dawson asked. "You can't make the entire fifteen hundred acres on horseback in a day."

"I'm well aware of the best way to patrol my ranch, but the chopper needs a new fuel gauge. Besides, my plan today was to ride the north ridge, not the entire property line."

Dawson let out an audible sigh. "Okay, lead the way."

"You don't have to come with me."

"I'm well aware of what I don't need to do," he said, parroting her words. "But this is serious, Sylvie. You could have died today."

"I know. I'll call the Beaverhead County Sheriff's office when I get back." She urged Fanny toward the trail.

"You must have some idea of who would do something like this," Dawson pressed as he fell in behind her. The trail wasn't wide enough for them to ride side by side.

"Funny you mention that, Dawson, because your ranch stands to benefit if something happens to me. Sean has made it clear he'd love nothing more than to sell McLane Mountain to your father or the next highest bidder. He wants to take the money and run."

"My old man can't afford to buy you out," Dawson said firmly. "I know our respective fathers have given each other the right of first refusal to buy the other's ranch when the time comes, but that doesn't mean zip if you don't have cash to cover the purchase. The Copper Creek Ranch is half the size of yours. If anyone would be the target, it would be you coming after me."

"I'd never do something like that." She glanced at him

over her shoulder. He looked good, too good. He was leaner than she remembered, but his recent surgeries likely played a role in that. Yet he still had the looks and the swagger she remembered. His dark hair was mostly covered by his cowboy hat, but his features were tan and rugged.

That stupid agreement their fathers had made thirty-eight years ago provided the motive for Dawson to shoot at her.

Instead, he'd saved her life.

Even more irksome than knowing someone else wanted her dead was the knowledge that she owed Dawson for what he'd done.

And Sylvie McLane always paid her debts.

THE WOMAN WAS DRIVING him insane. Dawson had planned a nice, leisurely ride until the gunfire had rung out, far closer than he'd liked. Diamond had reared at the sound too, but he'd managed to remain seated, despite the pull on his abdominal muscles. But then Sylvie had hit the ground, rolling toward the edge of the mountain.

Was it too much to ask that she head back to the ranch to be safe?

He'd interacted with several tough women in the military, and each of them could certainly hold their own in a male-dominated environment. Sylvie could too, but ironically, the military was more progressive than the Wild West. Sylvie carried a large chip on her shoulder, likely related to the macho cowboys who felt a woman's place was in the kitchen, barefoot and pregnant.

He tried not to imagine Sylvie in his kitchen, perhaps

barefoot and round with child. He wryly shook his head. She'd punch him in the nose for even thinking about it.

Their fathers had been close, but he and Sylvie hadn't seen that much of each other. She'd been homeschooled so that she could work the ranch. There were town gatherings where they'd run into each other, but they'd also kept busy with their respective ranch chores. Truth be told, twenty years ago, his main focus had been to graduate and join the military.

His dad had been disappointed but remained proud of what Dawson had accomplished. Not everyone made it through the rigorous BUD/S training to become a Navy SEAL. And now that Dawson was back home, his father made it clear he wanted to hand the ranch over to him.

A gift he didn't really want.

"There's a creek up ahead, we can stop there to water the horses," Sylvie said.

"Okay." There was no doubt in his mind she knew the mountain terrain better than he did. The hour was pushing noon, and his stomach rumbled with hunger.

The three surgeries to remove shrapnel had done a number on his overall strength and agility. Four months since the last surgery and he still didn't feel anywhere near 100 percent.

His SEAL team had run their last mission back in December. They'd successfully taken out their terrorist target, but the extraction had been a cluster. The underwater bomb that had been detonated while they were swimming to their extraction boat had killed their teammate, Jaydon Rampart.

The rest of the team had all sustained injuries of some sort, but they'd survived. Their Senior Chief, Mason Gray, had lost his hearing in one ear and suffered partial hearing loss in the other. Kaleb had completely blown out his knee; Hudd had lost vision in one eye and suffered a head injury that still plagued him. Dallas had taken shrapnel to his shoulder, while Nico had suffered a rupture of his Achilles tendon. In comparison, Dawson's abdominal injuries weren't that bad.

Yet he hated feeling weak and helpless. Pulling Sylvie up from where she'd dangled off the edge of the mountain had sent ripples of pain through his damaged muscles. Well worth it to save a life.

Which brought him back to the question of who would want Sylvie dead?

"You said there were too many to count." He pulled Diamond up beside her mare and slid out of the saddle. He bent to rub Kilo's fur, feeling bad for dragging the lab farther than intended.

He'd been about to turn back to the house when the gunshot had gone off.

"Your dad, your foreman, Max Wolfe, my foreman, Josh O'Leary, my brother, oh, and possibly my ex-husband." She led Fanny by the reins toward the creek. "Is that enough for you?"

"My dad isn't part of this, Sylvie." It ticked him off that she'd even considered his old man a threat. "He wants me to take over the Copper Creek Ranch. No way does he want the responsibility of yours too."

"Okay, fine. One less possible threat, then." She sighed, then added, "I'm sorry. I'm being grumpy over something that isn't your fault."

"At least you got that right," he muttered. He swept off his hat and wiped the sweat from his brow. "I'd feel better if you headed back to the homestead. This guy could be watching us through a rifle scope right now."

"I know, Dawson. But he could do that tomorrow or the next day too." She led Fanny away after the horse had finished drinking from the stream. He did the same with Diamond while Kilo drank some water, then stretched out on the grass, content to rest. "What am I supposed to do? Hire a bodyguard?"

It was on the tip of his tongue to offer to take on that role, then he remembered he needed to help run his father's ranch. Not that Max Wolfe, their foreman, wasn't perfectly capable of doing most of the work. Max had done all that and more while Dawson had been in the navy. Yet Sylvie's comment had him wondering about the guy.

Why would the foreman of the Copper Creek Ranch want to harm Sylvie? The only way that made sense was if Wolfe thought he would be next in line to take over his father's ranch, if Dawson decided to leave.

Had Wolfe learned of his conversations with his father?

Even if he had, why would the foreman want a second, much bigger ranch? The Cooper Creek was doing well, no reason to want more. Nah, the more he thought about it, the more he couldn't see the logic.

"I can help protect you as often as possible," he said. "I know we're both busy helping our fathers, but I don't want anything to happen to you."

She glanced at him in surprise. "I didn't realize you were taking over for your dad."

"I'm helping him out temporarily." He wished the ranch wasn't hanging like a yoke around his neck. "He fell and broke his hip a few months back. He's actually recovering fairly well, but he can't ride yet."

"Yeah, I know, your father and mine have been commiserating about their medical issues." Sylvie frowned. "It's tough, for both of them. I love riding, it's the best part of owning a ranch."

"Me too." Riding horseback was something he enjoyed, although he liked being in the water too. Which was why he wasn't thrilled about possibly sticking around in Montana, miles from the ocean. "We need to head back. I can't help feeling vulnerable out here without any indication of where the threat is coming from."

"Fine, we can head back, but I'd like to take a less traveled path to avoid being seen." She eyed him thoughtfully. "Are you hungry? I have two sandwiches and am happy to share."

"Ah, sure." He was touched by her offer. For once, Sylvie was attempting to be nice. "Thanks."

They sat on the ground across from each other. Kilo came over to curl up next to his side. Dawson stroked the dog as he ate.

"It's been an uphill battle since my dad's cancer diagnosis," Sylvie said. "I've taken over all the work, but the guys treat me like I'm some sort of impostor who knows nothing about ranching."

"Because they're cowboys." He waved his hand. "They're not really dissing you, Sylvie, it's just that they're used to taking orders from your father or Josh." He paused, then asked, "Why did you list your ex-husband as a possible suspect?"

Her cheeks went pink, and she didn't answer for a long moment. "Mostly because he'd go after the ranch out of revenge. The marriage wasn't working, he didn't like it that I was so involved in running the ranch."

"So what, he thought he should run it?"

"No, I think he figured my dad would run it while we just sat around and took in the profits." She scowled. "I soon realized I was happier outside doing ranch chores than being with him, so I told him to take a hike. He wasn't happy with me."

Ouch. Dawson could understand why. "What's his name?"

"Paul Griffin. Although I think he moved to Boulder, Colorado, so it may be a stretch to consider him a suspect."

"Shouldn't be too difficult to find out if that's really where he's living now."

"Maybe the gunfire was a poacher." Sylvie pursed her lips. "I mean, everyone out here knows how to shoot a gun, both handgun and rifle. I'm not that small of a target, and if the shooter was using a scope, they shouldn't have missed."

"His goal may have been to make it look like an accident," Dawson pointed out.

"Maybe. No one would have known the details if you hadn't been there to drag me up over the cliff." She balled up the paper sandwich wrapping and took his too, stashing them in the saddlebag. "We'll go down lizard trail, it's the long way to get back, but it should help keep us hidden from view."

"Whatever you think is best." He wasn't about to argue. This was her ranch, her land. Just looking at Sylvie with her dark hair pulled back from her face, minus the normal cowboy hat she wore, he knew ranching was in her blood.

It made him mad that someone wanted to take it from her.

He glanced at Kilo, debating whether he should carry the dog in his arms down lizard trail. "How steep is it? Will Kilo be okay?"

She hesitated, then nodded. "I think so. The horses will take it slow and easy. He looks like he'll be able to keep up."

"Okay, we'll see how it goes. If he struggles, then I'll carry him."

"Does Kilo like being carried while on the back of a horse?"

"Not particularly, but he'll do what I ask of him. That's the kind of dog he is." His training of Kilo had been somewhat hampered by his surgeries, but the canine still listened to Dawson's commands.

"Are you ready to roll?" Sylvie asked, brushing crumbs from her jeans.

"Sure." He stood too, reaching for Diamond's reins. "How long will it take to get to the bottom?"

"An hour, maybe more," she answered.

He rubbed his sore abdomen, trying not to groan loud enough for her to hear. He wasn't going to be the one to hold her back. If she wanted to take this route, that's what they'd do.

Sylvie took the lead. He had to smile at the image of her telling her husband to take a hike. It would take a strong man to handle her.

Not that he was vying for the chance. He preferred his life uncomplicated. Being a SEAL made having a relationship extremely difficult, but even now that he was out with his full pension, he was in no hurry to change his ways.

Maybe he was more like Sylvie than he wanted to admit.

She turned Fanny and headed down what he viewed as a treacherous trail. He kept one eye on Kilo and the other on Sylvie as they slowly descended the mountain.

He'd been home long enough to become accustomed to the altitude, but he still found himself feeling a bit breathless. Sylvie acted as if she were on a peaceful trail ride, swaying back and forth in the saddle like a natural.

He had to give her credit. The lady was one tough cowboy.

One of Diamond's hooves slipped on a rock. He gripped the gelding with his knees, and the animal quickly found his footing. Dawson breathed out a sigh of relief.

So far, Kilo was doing okay, but he still worried about the canine. This was one of the longest rides he'd taken the dog on, and he didn't want to harm the animal. Good thing Kilo was young enough to treat this like an exciting game. Every so often, the yellow lab would lift his snout to sniff the air, no doubt taking in all the interesting scents surrounding them.

Hopefully, the slower pace would prevent the dog from getting too tired and worn out. There were other hazards too, like snakes and other varmints.

They were about halfway down the mountainside when Kilo abruptly began to growl. He instinctively slid off Diamond just as he heard a rumbling noise. As he looked up, his heart squeezed in his chest when he saw a large boulder tipping off the edge of the cliff. If it continued its trajectory, it would come straight toward them.

"Sylvie! Look out!" Bending at the waist, he grabbed Kilo. The trail was so narrow, there wasn't much of an option to move the horse out of the way, but he did his best.

Holding Kilo to his chest, he plastered himself against the mountainside, hoping and praying the boulder would somehow miss them.

CHAPTER TWO

After sliding off Fanny, Sylvie urged the horse closer to the edge of the mountain, positioning herself in front of the mare. It was the only thing she could think of to prevent the large boulder from squashing them both. Not that she was much of a deterrent, but she didn't want her horse hurt.

The side of the rock grazed the side of her head and shoulder as it tumbled past. Sylvie winced in pain, standing frozen for several long moments as she willed her heart rate to return to normal.

"Sylvie! Talk to me! Are you okay?" Dawson's shout spurred her into action. He had been behind her, hence higher on the trail than she and Fanny. When she saw him standing there beside Diamond, cradling his large dog to his chest, her heart turned to mush as she realized he'd attempted to protect his animals the same way she had.

"Yes, thankfully." She fingered the side of her head, then the rip along her short-sleeved T-shirt. The boulder had scrapped off a layer of skin, but the injury could have been worse.

Much worse.

"Stay where you are," Dawson said. She noticed he'd lost his hat the way she'd lost hers during her roll toward the edge of the cliff. "We're coming down to meet you."

"Okay." It wasn't a hardship to wait for him, her body was trembling from the near impact of the boulder.

If the shooter's goal was to scare her, he was succeeding better than she cared to admit. Was Dawson right about someone trying to hurt her by making it look like an accident?

Rocks slid down the mountains all the time. More so in spring when the earth was thawing after a long winter. Not so much in June.

"Easy, girl." Stroking Fanny's head and neck helped calm them both. She let out a long breath. She needed to get to the sheriff, sooner rather than later.

Although what could he do about a nameless and face-less threat? Absolutely nothing.

Dawson carried Kilo as he led Diamond down the trail toward her. The lab was gangly but seemed content in his owner's arms. She noticed a slight grimace when Dawson finally set the dog on his feet. "Are you hurt?"

"No." She lightly touched the scrape along the side of her head. "Just bruised."

Dawson stared up at the steep cliffside above them. "That was no accident."

"I know." She didn't follow his gaze, turning instead toward the trail. They were still far from the ranch house. Better to push forward. "Let's walk for a bit."

"Fine." Dawson sounded angry, and she couldn't blame him.

They walked in silence for ten minutes. She cast her gaze up the mountain to make sure there weren't additional untoward surprises in store for them.

"Does your ex-husband have the ability to shoot and loosen a boulder?"

She glanced over her shoulder. "Yeah, he knows the layout of the place well enough. Paul worked the ranch for a year before we got engaged."

"We can find out easily enough where your foreman and mine were when these incidents happened," Dawson said.

"Having an alibi doesn't mean much," she pointed out. "Max or Josh could have hired someone to do the deed."

"There has to be a way to figure out who is behind these threats," Dawson insisted. "Especially if they continue to escalate."

He wasn't telling her anything she hadn't already figured out for herself. To be fair, she figured her ex-husband or Josh were the two main suspects. Josh had not been happy when she and Paul began seeing each other, then got married. She'd known Josh had a crush on her, but she didn't have those sorts of feelings toward him.

As it turned out, Josh may have been the better choice. Or not, if he turned out to be the mastermind behind these attacks.

The whole thing made her head hurt.

"How is your dad doing?"

She shrugged. "He's okay. The biggest issue is that the chemo makes him sick and weak. As I said, the worst part is that, like your dad, he hasn't been able to ride since his prostate surgery."

"Ouch," Dawson muttered. "I bet that hurt."

She rolled her eyes. "No worse than giving birth, I'm sure."

"You have a child?"

"No!" She could feel her cheeks getting red. "I'm just

saying men are big babies about that sort of thing when women are just supposed to pop out a kid." She tried to think of a different subject. "What about you? Is there a wife and kids waiting for you back in San Diego?"

"Nope. Never been married. It's just me and Kilo."

The news shouldn't have made her secretly relieved. And happy. When she'd signed the divorce papers, she'd vowed never to get hitched again. Dealing with men wasn't worth the time or energy. Especially when she didn't have much of either to spare.

So why this sudden awareness of Dawson Steele? A man she barely knew? They'd been neighbors, sure, but there was a four-year age gap between them. Besides, she'd been homeschooled around ranch chores, so it wasn't as if they'd seen each other often. He'd joined the military before she was remotely interested in boys.

A late bloomer, her dad had called her. He wasn't wrong.

"I can see your place." When she glanced back at Dawson, he was gesturing toward the dark brown, sprawling ranch house nestled in the valley below.

"I know." His ranch was located on the other side of Copper Creek. She'd been there a handful of times over the past twenty years, but not often.

Ranchers helped each other in times of need, but that rarely meant being inside each other's homes. Instead, they'd likely be helping with rogue cattle or horses, maybe pulling together to clear properties after vicious storms.

In that moment she realized Dawson had likely never been inside her home, despite the fact that his father's ranch butted up against her property. He'd been at the ranch often enough, borrowed her chopper a few months ago, but that didn't include going inside the home she shared with her dad.

They managed to reach the ranch house without any more trouble. As she and Dawson rode in, Josh stepped out from the barn. She watched him closely, searching for any indication that he was behind the attacks. "Josh."

"Sylvie. You're back earlier than expected."

"Yep." She didn't bother to enlighten him. She hid a grimace as she slid off Fanny.

"Something happen?" Josh glanced at Dawson, then back at her. "You have a scrape along the side of your shoulder."

"I'm fine." She wasn't about to confide in the foreman. Not yet. She glanced at Dawson who was also standing beside Diamond. "Dawson, you remember Josh O'Leary?"

"I do," Dawson said with a nod.

"Steele. What brings you to McLane Mountain?" Josh asked. Was there a note of suspicion in his tone?

"Chance meeting with Sylvie, that's all," Dawson said.

"Let's take the horses inside, give them some time to rest." Sylvie tugged Fanny toward the barn.

"I can do that for you," Josh began, but she cut him off.

"I always take care of my own ride." Ignoring Josh's affronted look, she led Fanny away. In truth, her entire body ached, and she would have loved nothing more than to hand the mare off to him. Except she feared that would only add to the theory that she was nothing but a weak woman. Besides, her horse was her responsibility.

Something her father had drilled into her when she was old enough to ride.

Josh muttered something she couldn't make out as she and Dawson moved past. When they reached the barn, Dawson said, "He's not a happy man."

"Not since Dad's cancer diagnosis," she agreed. "He's fifteen years younger than my dad, but I suspect it's the knowing we're all mere mortals spending time here only temporarily that has gotten to him." She led Fanny into her stall, gesturing to the empty one next to it for Diamond. "Add to that how Josh expected to take over the ranch from my father one day, only to learn I'm the one who'll be in charge, you get one cranky cowboy."

"I see that," Dawson drawled. "Looks to me like you're living in a nest of snakes."

His exaggerated western drawl made her smile. "All except for my dad."

His gaze turned serious. "You need to let your dad know what's going on."

"No. I don't want to worry him. He has enough on his plate while undergoing his cancer treatments."

Thankfully, Dawson didn't push the issue. They cared for the horses in silence, and once the horses had been brushed and watered, they trudged up to the house. There was no sign of Josh now, which was fine with her. While they'd worked in the barn, Kilo had stretched out to rest, but now the dog had regained some of his previous energy, trotting next to Dawson as they walked.

"Would you like something to drink?" She tried to think of what was in the fridge. "I have lemonade and iced tea."

"Whatever you're having would be great." Dawson gazed around at the house as she led him into the kitchen. "Nice place, roomy yet cozy at the same time. You going to call the sheriff's department? I can hang out here to help give my side of the story."

She sighed and nodded. After filling two glasses of lemonade and handing him one, she dropped into the closest kitchen chair and pulled out her phone. "I'll call, but

I doubt this will be a priority for them. No need for you to hang around."

"I'll wait." His tone held an edge that made her think it wouldn't be easy to force him to go. Normally, she'd be irritated.

After the two near misses, his stubbornness was a relief.

She waited for the dispatcher to answer the call. "This is Sylvie McLane. I'd like to report an incident of gunfire on the north ridge of my property, which almost cost me my life. As well as a possible second attack."

"My goodness, Sylvie, are you okay?" It took a moment for the female voice to register, then Sylvie realized it was Brenda Eastman, a woman who had dated one of her cowboys for a while.

"I'm fine, Brenda, don't worry. My reason for reporting these incidents is to have them on record in case they continue." She paused, then added, "Will you ask Marty to call me?"

"Of course, hun. I'll either have Marty or Chief Deputy Rick give you a call. Rick will probably get to you first; the sheriff has been tied up in meetings. Is this your cell?"

"Yes." Sylvie waited for Brenda to make note of her number. "Thanks again."

"Take care, Sylvie."

She disconnected from the call and tossed the phone onto the table. "Either Sheriff Marty Cline or his chief deputy, Rick Holmes, will call me back. Would you like a ride back to your ranch? We can load Diamond into a horse trailer."

"No thanks." Dawson sipped his lemonade. "I'll wait until someone calls back."

She stared at him. "And what if that doesn't happen until tomorrow?"

He shrugged and glanced down at Kilo. "I have some food for Kilo in my saddlebags. We can hang out for as long as it takes." He met her gaze. "I'm not leaving you alone with the snakes, Sylvie. So don't bother to argue."

"Fine." She reluctantly rose to her feet. "I'll set up one of the guest rooms. Nothing fancy for dinner, but there's plenty of chili and cornbread."

"I love chili and cornbread."

She wryly shook her head, knowing his response would have been the same no matter what she'd told him they were having for dinner.

It was wrong to be relieved to have Dawson nearby since she knew it couldn't last. But there was no denying he made her feel safe.

The snakes, as he described them, could strike at any time.

SYLVIE WAS A CONTRADICTION. Tough when it came to running her ranch yet potentially naïve when it came to men. Oh, she'd been married, but it was clear the guy had only wanted the McLane ranch. Or rather the profits from it, not the actual work itself.

While she went to the guest room, he went back out to the barn to get Kilo's food from his pack. Good thing Navy SEALs prided themselves on always being prepared. He returned to the kitchen with Kilo at his side. The dog kept looking up at him expectantly, knowing it was dinnertime.

He finished feeding Kilo by the time she returned from the guest room. When she began pulling food out of the fridge, he frowned. "Don't you have help? You can't manage the house and the entire ranch alone."

"We normally have Rhonda Joseph who comes in to cook and clean. She's married to Hector, one of the older ranch hands. But Rhonda and Hector are visiting their first grandchild this week, so we've been winging it." A rueful smile creased her features. "Hence the simple meal. I learned a lot about ranching from my dad, but cooking is not my best skill."

He nodded and twisted to get out of her way, hiding a wince. Man, he was sick of his abdominal muscles hurting. The surgeon had said that the pain would recede at some point, but he was beginning to think this was his new normal. That the pain would never completely go away. "I'll help. Tell me what you need."

"It's all ready, we're just heating it up." A smile tugged at her features. "I probably should have mentioned that we're eating leftovers."

"I love leftovers." He knew from helping his dad run their smaller ranch that keeping the house up and the ranch running smoothly was a lot of work. He admired the way Sylvie simply did what was necessary without complaining.

He may have judged her too harshly a few months ago. He'd been in a time crunch and had needed to borrow her chopper to get to Boise, Idaho, to help one of his SEAL teammates. She hadn't been happy to loan him the bird, but then she relented, bluntly telling him she expected it back by the end of the day, fully fueled, and that if there were any mechanical issues, she'd expect him to pay for them.

He'd followed her instructions to the letter. Something she'd barely acknowledged when he'd set the chopper down on their landing pad.

Now he understood how stressed she was with her father's illness and the lack of respect she was getting from her ranch foreman and the other guys working for her. It clearly hasn't been an easy road.

After Sylvie filled large bowls with chili, he manned the microwave. Kilo stood next to him, but when he frowned at the dog, the animal went to stretch out beneath the table. Kilo knew better than to beg for food. "Where's your dad?"

"He's not feeling well, so he fixed himself some toast earlier." She frowned. "The chemo has really done a number on his appetite. He's lost forty pounds since his diagnosis."

"I'm sorry to hear that." Dawson glanced at her. "I'll keep you and your dad in my prayers."

She glanced at him in surprise but didn't say anything. Maybe she thought that was just a phrase, but he meant it. Being part of the SEAL team had brought him close to death on more than one occasion. Like their last op that had gone sideways. He'd made his peace with God, thanks to Kaleb, who had always shared his view on God and faith.

During his surgeries, he'd prayed often. Maybe God's grace was the reason he was here today. He was very glad he'd been out riding Diamond when the gunfire had sounded, when Sylvie had busted off her ride. God was watching over her, too, whether she realized it or not.

When their chili was hot, Sylvie added white cheddar cheese to their bowls, then added large squares of cornbread. He took a seat next to her at the table.

"I'd like to say grace," he said.

"Ah, okay." He could tell his request caught her off guard.

He wanted to reach over to take her hand but feared she'd slug him. So he simply bowed his head. "Lord, we thank You for this wonderful food we are about to eat. We also thank You for keeping us safe in Your care today. Amen."

Sylvie didn't say anything for a long moment. "Do you always do that? Or was the prayer for my benefit?"

"Almost always," he said. "We didn't pray earlier when we ate our sandwiches. To be honest, I forgot." He shrugged. "No one is perfect."

"That's true." She dug in to her chili with relish. "My dad has become a believer since his diagnosis. Says the hospital chaplain spoke to him about God."

"I'm glad." He eyed her thoughtfully. "But not you?"

She flushed and took a bite of the cornbread. After a moment, she shrugged. "I haven't had time to think about it. It's been all I can do to keep things running smoothly around here."

"God can help ease your burdens," he said. "Not physically coming to help but emotionally. I leaned on God a lot during my surgeries."

"You don't have to tell me, but I'm curious as to why you'd need so many abdominal surgeries. Did something happen when you were a Navy SEAL?"

"I took a load of shrapnel in my gut on our last mission." He met her gaze. "The problem is that when bowel gets nicked, there's a lot of potential for infection. Which is what happened to me. After the first two surgeries, I thought I was fine, but then another piece of shrapnel was found on a follow-up X-ray, and it embedded itself in my small bowel, so the whole process started over again."

"Wow, that must have been difficult."

"I survived." When Jaydon hadn't, he silently added. "The biggest problem is that the procedures prevented me from coming home sooner. I had to stick close to the VA hospital in San Diego."

"Is that where you live?"

"I had a place there during my years in the navy," he admitted. "Haven't decided where I'll put down roots with Kilo now that I'm out."

"Being out of the military must give you a new sense of freedom."

"Sort of, but I miss the camaraderie of my teammates." Something he'd only realized a couple of months ago when he'd flown to Boise to meet up with Kaleb and to help Hudd. "And I have my dad to consider."

"Yeah." She stared at her bowl of chili for a moment. "I've always known I'd live and die here on McLane Mountain."

"You don't have to keep the ranch going," he felt compelled to point out.

"Now you sound like my brother, Sean." There was an edge to her tone. "He'd like nothing more than for me to sell so he can get his half of the money to live wherever he wants."

"I'm not trying to take sides, Sylvie. You sounded as if you were stuck here, and you're not."

"Of course, I'm not. I like ranching. It's what I've worked for my entire life. Sean could help, but he chooses not to." She waved her spoon. "Never mind, let's change the subject. Thinking of Sean makes me cranky."

"Speaking of which, where is he?"

"No clue. Left two weeks ago to stay with a friend." She snorted. "I've stopped giving him money, told him if he's not going to work the ranch, he doesn't get paid. I have no idea what he's living on, I can only hope he found a job."

Interesting. "Sounds as if Sean could have easily fired that shot at you today and loosened the boulder."

She closed her eyes for a moment, then nodded. "Yes.

He could have. I don't want to believe he'd do something like that. Like I said earlier, there are too many possible suspects to consider."

"We'll make a list and see if we can account for everyone's whereabouts." Dawson wasn't a detective, but the navy had taught him how to use intel to his advantage. Kilo shifted beneath the table, and he smiled when the dog began to snore softly. "Once we do that, we'll have something to give to the sheriff's department."

"Why not." She sounded exhausted, and he couldn't blame her. It must be awful to know that someone close to her had tried to harm her.

Would have killed her if he hadn't been there to pull her up over the edge of the cliff.

They ate in silence for a few moments. He liked the kick of the chili cooled by the corn bread. "You're not giving yourself enough credit, Sylvie. This is delicious. Your chili is better than anything I've tasted before."

Her smile was wry. "Thanks, but man cannot live on chili alone. When we're finished here, I'd like to check on the horses."

"Understood." It occurred to him he should call his dad to let him know he was at the McLane ranch. It wasn't easy to go back to living with a parent after being mostly out of touch while in the navy for twenty years. But he didn't want his dad to worry. "I'll wash the dishes."

"Are you for real?" Sylvie glared at him suspiciously. "Men never offer to do dishes. Why are you being so nice?"

Dumbfounded, he stared at her. "When haven't I been nice to you?"

"You haven't been mean exactly, except when you told me I should dress like a girl so people wouldn't think I was a boy. But it seems like you're going out of your way to be nice."

He vaguely remembered her as a preteen—tall, skinny, and gangly. The tips of his ears burned with shame as he remembered their chance meeting outside the ice-cream shop in Dillon. To his stupid teenage eyes, she'd looked more like a boy than a girl. "I'm sorry, but I was a dumb fifteen-year-old."

"And I was an eleven-year-old tomboy. Don't worry, I'm over it." She finished her chili and cornbread, then stood. "Let's check on the horses first. The dishes can wait."

He carried his dishes to the sink and filled them with water to soak. "Come, Kilo."

The dog woke up from his nap, stretched, then trotted over to join them. He followed Sylvie outside, enjoying the cool June breeze coming off the mountains.

It was much colder here in Montana than San Diego. Snowstorms in June were not uncommon. Yet the scenery was beautiful. He liked the mountains, almost as much as he enjoyed the ocean.

"You have some really nice horses," he said as they walked down the center of the horse barn. "My dad always talked about how well your dad knew horses."

"I've been doing some horse training to broaden our income base." She glanced at him. "We had to cut back on our beef cattle to preserve the land. Figured horses could make up the difference. And it would have if my dad hadn't gotten sick."

"It does seem like a never-ending battle to keep the ranch going."

"I don't care, I'm not selling. Especially not to those big investment groups. You think cattle ranching will ruin the land? Wait until those greedy jerks take the land and use if for commercial property."

"Whoa, I wasn't suggesting you should." He hadn't intended to hit her hot button. "I think you're doing a great job."

"How would you know?"

"My dad says you are, and I'm sure he's been in touch with your dad."

Sylvie blew out a breath. "Sorry, I guess the events of the day have gotten to me. You're right, your dad has been here several times. My dad is grateful for the company."

"I'll let him know. Speaking of which, I need to call him." He reached into his pocket for his phone when he caught a flash of movement from the corner of his eye. It took a nanosecond for his mind to realize a pitchfork was sailing toward them. He instinctively pushed Sylvie out of the way, lifting his arm to deflect the missile.

The fork clattered to the ground with a loud metallic sound. He raked a glance over Sylvie, glad to note the sharp tines had missed her. Then a flash of anger had him spinning around and sprinting toward the location where the fork had come from.

He couldn't wait to get his hands on the guy who'd tried to hurt Sylvie for the third time!

CHAPTER THREE

Plastered up against the side of Fanny's stall, Sylvie stared in shock as the pitchfork hit the ground in the spot where she had been standing a few seconds ago. Once again, Dawson had come to her rescue.

Maybe she did need a bodyguard.

Dawson had taken off running down the center aisle of the barn, with Kilo hot on his heels. She pulled herself together and followed, equally determined not to let the person who'd done this get away scot-free.

She checked each stall along the way but didn't see a single person, just horses. By the time she joined Dawson outside, he looked frustrated. Kilo was running back and forth in front of him as if this might be a new game.

"Which way would he go?" Dawson asked impatiently.

Feeling helpless, she shook her head. "There's no way to know."

For long moments they did nothing but look around the area outside the barn. A tall man wearing a cowboy hat came into view, leading a horse. As he came closer, she recognized their ranch foreman, Josh O'Leary.

"Do you think he's the one who did this?" Dawson asked in a low voice.

"Doubtful. There wouldn't have been time for him throw the fork, get out of the barn, and get all the way around the corral."

"I'm not sure I agree," Dawson said. "If he had the horse behind the barn, he could have made it in time."

"Maybe." She still thought it wasn't likely. Yet at the same time, she wasn't willing to take anyone off the suspect list.

Not yet.

"Hey Sylvie," Josh greeted her as he came closer. He lifted a brow upon seeing Dawson. "Steele, you're still here? Is there some sort of problem?"

"No problem, Sylvie invited me to dinner," Dawson responded. "Where are you coming from?"

Josh looked surprised by his question. "Had to fix a section of fence out on the south end of the pasture. Why? Did something happen?"

The way he asked about something happening made the tiny hairs on the back of her neck rise. It wasn't something Josh would normally inquire about. She wondered if he'd purposely made sure to have an alibi when the incident had gone down.

Paranoid much? Oh yeah.

When she sensed Dawson was going to respond in the affirmative, she put a hand on his arm and quickly interjected, "Of course not. Dawson and I were just about to check on the horses."

A flash of annoyance crossed Josh's features. "I can do that, Sylvie."

"So can I." She didn't point out that it was her ranch and therefore her responsibility. She turned toward

Dawson. "Ready?"

"Sure."

She led the way inside and quickly moved down to where the pitchfork was lying on the ground. She grabbed it from the floor and propped it against the side of the stall before Josh could see.

There were always ranch hands roaming around, but it had struck her as odd that they hadn't seen anyone when they'd first entered the barn. Josh could very well have been fixing a section of fence, although that begged the question of why he'd taken on the task rather than delegating it to one of the other ranch hands.

A shiver rippled down her spine. Obviously she was a target, but the attempts being done from afar made it difficult to figure out who was behind them.

The pitchfork incident had been the closest. She turned to scan the interior of the barn again. They'd come down the center aisle, but there were some double stalls that could have provided cover.

Had they missed something? Was someone still hiding inside the barn?

"Easy, Storm," Josh said as he led the stallion into the barn. The horse was her father's pride and joy, a beautiful creature although he was getting on in years. Storm had sired many a foal, several with Fanny. Sylvie often rode Storm, but not up in the mountains.

No reason to be irked that Josh had taken the stallion out. Although then again, it was odd that the foreman had taken the prize stallion to fix a fence.

They had plenty of work horses for just that purpose.

She was so lost in her thoughts she walked into Dawson. He lightly grasped her shoulders to steady her. "Are you okay?" He kept his voice low so Josh couldn't hear.

The warmth of his palms on her shoulders was unnerving. She told herself to ignore the sensation and shrugged. What could she say? The pitchfork hadn't touched her, and looking back, she could easily assume it had been used to scare her rather than to kill her.

Yet it was the third such event in the past eight hours.

She didn't even want to imagine what tomorrow might bring.

"We need to talk to your father," Dawson said. "This is ridiculous."

"No need to worry him." She had hoped to hear from the sheriff's office by now. "We can talk more later." She nodded toward the stall where Josh was caring for Storm, indicating she didn't want to discuss it with him.

After several minutes, Josh left the barn. Sylvie went up and down the main aisle again, looking for anything she may have missed.

But she didn't find anything.

"I don't get it," she told Dawson. "What is the point of all this? To scare me into selling?"

"Maybe, because the pitchfork seemed a pathetic attempt to hurt you at best. Hang on a minute." Dawson pulled out his phone and took several steps away as he used it. Not so far that she couldn't hear his side of the conversation. "Dad? Hey, I ran into Sylvie earlier, so I'm at the McLane ranch. Yeah, I'll tell him you say hi. Listen, I'm probably going to bunk here tonight, unless you need me for something?" There was a pause before he said, "Okay, I'll call you in the morning."

She wanted to tell him he didn't need to stay, but the

words wouldn't emerge from her throat. The truth was, she wanted him to. Maybe it was just a holdover from the way he'd saved her life when she nearly went off the edge of the cliff, but she knew she'd sleep better knowing Dawson was right down the hall in the guest room.

"All set," Dawson said, shoving the phone back into his pocket.

"Thanks, Dawson. For everything." She offered a wan smile. "I'm sorry I accused you of firing the rifle at me."

"Hey, don't worry about it." He frowned. "Seems to me you have a reason to be suspicious. I don't like what's happening here, Sylvie."

"Me either." She gave Fanny a pat, then turned away. "Come on, we should head inside. I'll take you to see Dad as long as you promise not to worry him about these events. I'm sure I'll hear from the sheriff's office soon."

Dawson stood for a moment, glancing around the barn before nodding. "Okay."

She carried the pitchfork back to the tack area near the front of the barn. The place was empty now and had been when they'd run out in search of the person who'd thrown it like a javelin. But as she hung it back on the wall, she tried to imagine Josh doing something like that.

It wasn't his style. Then again, the ranch was worth over twenty-five million including the house, the barn, and other outbuildings, along with the livestock, if she and her dad decided to put the place on the market.

That kind of money could turn anyone into a criminal.

Yet there were other ranches on the market, priced equally high, that were not selling. The ranch was only worth what someone was willing to pay for it. And in lean times, those prospects were slim.

Ranching was hard work, without a whole lot of reward. It wasn't like people were flocking from the city to take up the ranching life.

Well, she would, but Sylvie knew she was an anomaly. Her brother certainly had chosen to escape the ranch life.

As she went inside the ranch house, she couldn't help feeling disheartened at the likely possibility Sean was the mastermind behind these attempts.

And to be honest, her suspicions were the main reason she didn't want to mention the incidents to her father.

DAWSON WAS INWARDLY SHOCKED at how frail Connor McLane was compared to the last time he'd seen him. He wished his father had warned him of the seriousness of Connor's condition, but he did his best not to show his reaction on his features.

"Mr. McLane, how are you?" Dawson took the older man's proffered hand. "This is my dog, Kilo."

"Call me Connor," Sylvie's dad said, waving his hand. "I've known you since you were a baby, and we don't stand on ceremony around here. Nice to see you and Kilo. How is your father? I haven't seen Landon in a couple of weeks."

"He's good, thanks." *Much better than Connor's condition*, he thought wryly. "I'm sure he'll stop by again soon."

"Yeah, I don't get out as often as I used to," Connor admitted.

Dawson could only imagine what the guy had been through. He cleared his throat and glanced at Sylvie who was watching him like an eagle about to scoop up its prey. After seeing her father's debilitated condition, he could understand why she didn't want him to worry, so he'd honor her wishes about not mentioning the attacks. At least, for now. "I'll make sure my dad swings by soon."

"Thanks, Dawson." Connor grinned. "Heard you were some hotshot Navy SEAL."

"I was a SEAL, yes. But I retired earlier this year. Came back to visit my dad and to train Kilo here." No doubt his dad has bragged about him to Connor, but he didn't want to talk about himself. "Sylvie is doing a great job with the ranch."

"She is," Connor agreed, eyeing his daughter with pride. "I'm blessed to have her."

"We're blessed to have each other," Sylvie corrected. "Can I get you anything, Dad? Are you hungry?"

"No thanks, I grabbed some leftovers earlier." The older man shifted in his recliner. "I'm fine, really."

Dawson wasn't sure about that, but he didn't voice his concern. "I need to take Kilo out but wanted to stop in to say hello. Take care, sir, I'll see you later."

"You too, Dawson."

"Good night, Dad." Sylvie went over to kiss her father's cheek. "Try to get some rest."

"That's all I've been doing lately," Connor groused. "Good night."

After leaving Connor's master suite, he asked, "Are you sure your dad is okay?"

"According to the doc, he should recover fully. They took out the cancer and have treated him aggressively." She grimaced. "He still has a couple of radiation treatments yet, and after that, it's building up his strength back to where it was before all this."

"That's for sure." He hesitated, then said, "You didn't

mention to him about my plan to stay in the guest room tonight."

"No, because he would assume there's something personal going on between us." He had to give her credit, she didn't beat around the bush. She arched her brow. "Neither one of us wants that."

The idea wasn't as distasteful as it should have been. Dawson forced himself to nod. "Right, I understand. I'll step outside for a few minutes to let Kilo out."

"Okay." She gestured toward the door.

He walked the canine outside, and Kilo eagerly watered a few trees, then did his business. After cleaning up after his dog, he disposed of the waste in the trash cans outside the spacious four-car garage.

When he and Kilo went back inside, he heard Sylvie's phone ring. She rolled her eyes and showed him the screen so he could see the caller was from the Beaverhead County Sheriff's Department. She put the call on speaker and held the phone in the palm of her hand. "This is Sylvie McLane."

"Sylvie, this is Rick Holmes from the sheriff's department. I hope I'm not calling too late."

Dawson scowled. Was this guy for real? He was treating Sylvie as if she were an old woman.

"Of course not, thanks for calling Rick. I need to report a couple of incidents that took place today."

"Yes, Brenda told me. Something about gunfire on your property? We can let the DNR know if you think there are poachers out there."

Dawson had to bite his tongue to prevent himself from snapping at the guy. Thankfully, Sylvie could handle her own.

"The gunfire was intended for me, Rick," she said firmly. "Fanny reared and busted me off. I was close to the edge of the cliff and nearly went over. Thankfully, Dawson Steele from the Copper Creek was close enough to lend me a hand."

"Dawson witnessed the incident?" Finally, Rick seemed to take her seriously.

"Yes, and about two hours later, a large boulder came crashing down on us as we descended the lizard trail. The last event happened in the barn just an hour ago, when someone threw a pitchfork like a javelin toward me. Thankfully, both the boulder and the pitchfork missed, but I need every one of these events well documented in your files in case this yahoo tries again."

"Yes, absolutely. That certainly sounds suspicious," Rick agreed. Suddenly the guy sounded anxious to appease her. "I can come out tomorrow morning to get all the details down on paper if that works for you. Any idea who would do this to you?"

"I have a lot of ideas. I'll fill you in tomorrow. Make it midmorning, say ten thirty," Sylvie said. "That'll give me time to take care of the horses."

"Sure thing, ten thirty is fine. See you then, Sylvie." The call ended.

"Idiot." Sylvie sighed. "He was ready to blow off my concerns until he knew you were a witness." She stared at the phone as if she wanted to chuck it across the room, and he didn't blame her. If this was the treatment she'd been getting from Josh and the other cowboys, then it was no wonder she carried a chip on her shoulder.

"I'm sorry he treated you like that, Sylvie. But the good news is that he will clearly take these threats seriously."

"Yeah, thanks to you." She waved a hand. "Sorry, I shouldn't be so jaded."

"I don't blame you," he said quietly. "You have every right to be upset."

"Yeah, well, it doesn't matter much either way. I don't have much faith in Chief Deputy Rick Holmes's ability to figure out who is behind these attacks."

"Maybe I can help." He blurted the offer before he realized what he was saying. "I mean, I'm not a computer expert or anything, but I'm sure I can do some searching on your brother as a starting point. Once we know if he has an alibi, we can move on from there."

Her gaze softened. "Thanks, Dawson, but you have your dad's ranch to worry about. It's not fair for me to take up your time with my problems."

"I'll find a way to do both," he insisted. Although, to be fair, his training was better suited to being a bodyguard rather than a detective. "Do you have a computer I can borrow?"

"Sure." She led the way to a large office located not far from the kitchen. He figured it had been the place where her father had run the ranch, but he could see she'd added a few feminine touches, scented candles and a bowl of wildflowers, to make it her own. There was a large computer sitting on the desk, but then off to the side there was a laptop tucked into a docking station. She removed the device and handed it to him. Kilo sat at his side, waiting patiently for them to be finished.

"Is there a password?"

She took a moment to jot a series of random numbers and letters on a sticky note. "Here you go."

"I'm impressed. Most people use their name, date of birth, etc. to form a password."

"I changed it after Sean left." She frowned. "I needed to make sure he couldn't access the bank accounts."

"I'm sorry you had to do that." He couldn't imagine being in a position where you couldn't trust your own brother. Dawson's SEAL teammates were like brothers to him, and he'd trusted each of them to cover his six multiple times over the past twenty years. "Thanks. Kilo and I will head to the guest room, but I'll let you know if I find anything useful."

"Don't work too long, you should get some sleep." She shut down the lights in the office and led him back to the main living area.

"I won't. Good night, Sylvie." He wished he had the right to kiss her.

"Good night, Dawson."

They returned to the hallway that housed the bedrooms. The McLane ranch home was all one level, sprawled across the land. He had to admit the place was very nice and larger than his father's home.

Yet it was also interesting that the only two people living there at the moment were Sylvie and Connor. He supposed Rhonda and her husband, Hector, usually lived there too.

Still, the many bedrooms, five by his count, begged for children. Not that he was interested in starting a family at his age. Thirty-nine felt ancient after his multiple abdominal surgeries.

Sylvie was only thirty-five, so she had time to have children if she so desired. Not likely now that she'd kicked her ex to the curb.

Which reminded him of his plan to try to find Paul Griffin, after he did some digging into Sylvie's brother.

Kilo sniffed around the room, then stretched out on the

rug next to the bed. Dawson sat with his back against the headboard. He wasn't an expert in using social media, but it didn't take him long to find Sean McLane's page. The privacy settings weren't engaged, so he could freely review the content.

Unfortunately, the guy didn't post very often. The last time was a month ago, at some rodeo in Butte, Montana, where he proudly displayed his winning belt buckle. The event was two weeks before Sean had apparently left the ranch to stay with a friend.

As he searched the photo, though, he found two other guys next to Sean, which he'd helpfully tagged, Matt Keagan and Ned Burns. Possibly one of the friends Sean was supposedly staying with.

If he wasn't hiding out on the ranch, tormenting his sister.

After an hour, he had some idea of where to find both Keagan and Burns. But his eyes were growing heavy, and his muscles were feeling stiff. Not uncommon since his surgeries, but annoying just the same.

He forced himself to start the search for Sylvie's ex, Paul Griffin. There were several Paul Griffins on social media, but he realized he had no idea what the guy looked like.

Setting the computer aside, he considered heading back down to Sylvie's office to see if she'd kept a picture of Paul there. Although why she would, he had no clue. She didn't strike him as the sentimental type. Especially not when she was the one who'd ended the marriage.

He returned to the computer screen, pulling up each photograph of the Paul Griffins in the mountain region. One of the five guys was much older, in his late forties, so he decided to scrap that one.

He was left with four possibilities now. Each of the four Paul Griffins were young and relatively nice-looking guys in their midthirties. He told himself there was no reason to be jealous of a man Sylvie had kicked out of her life.

Finally, Dawson gave up and closed the computer. He turned off the lamp and stripped down to his boxers and T-shirt.

The moment his head hit the pillow, he was down for the count.

"Move! We have tangos on our tail!"

Dawson didn't need the senior chief to tell him that, he could feel the bullets whizzing past him. If they were better shots, he'd be dead.

They'd all be dead.

He saw the sanctuary of the ocean looming before them. Senior Chief Mason Gray didn't hesitate to seek refuge in the salty depths. Dawson and the others quickly followed his lead. He swam underwater for a long time, only coming up for air when absolutely necessary. Every time Dawson's head broke the surface, gunfire rang out, forcing him to go under again.

They were moving toward the rig located a solid two miles off the coast. They were only at the halfway point when the bomb went off.

Jaydon's position had been farthest to the left, and when the explosion rocked the ocean, Dawson had been thrown head over butt in the water. He hadn't realized he'd taken a load of shrapnel to his belly until he managed to get himself upright and to the surface. Then the pain had been staggering, but he'd ignored it while trying to do a head count.

The team had to stick together. They had to!

"Where's Jay?" Mason shouted.

They were a man short. Each of them instantly dove

beneath the surface to try to find their buddy. But it was dark and impossible to see anything in the gritty, churned water.

Dawson went up for air to see Nico and Hudd holding on to Jay. He swam toward them, only to realize Jay wasn't conscious.

"We have to do CPR!" Nico shouted.

No easy task while in the water, but as a team, they managed. They worked on Jaydon for what seemed like hours but was likely only twenty minutes.

Unfortunately without success.

Jaydon was dead.

Dawson sat bolt upright in bed, his heart pounding in his chest as he relived those fateful moments their mission had turned deadly. His stomach muscles ached, and he realized he must have been twisting and turning in the bed.

He swung his feet over the edge, taking care to avoid stepping on Kilo still sleeping on the floor next to his bed. He lowered his head into his hands for a moment, then eased upright and tugged on his jeans.

Kilo woke up, and he inwardly grimaced. The lab began to whine, giving him little choice but to take him outside.

"You're a pain, you know that?" He eyed the dog as he pulled on his shoes.

Kilo went over to the door and began to growl low in his throat. The growling was new, and he tried to hush the animal lest he wake Sylvie and Connor.

When he opened the door, though, he smelled it too.

Smoke.

Dawson bolted down the hall, his gaze searching for the source of the smoke. Where were the smoke alarms anyway? Shouldn't they be going off?

Then he realized the smoke was outside. The barn!

"Sylvie!" He pounded on her bedroom door. "Fire in

the barn!" Then without waiting, he bolted outside. Time was of the essence, there would be no city fire engine response.

And if the fire got out of control, it could spread into a huge wildfire covering the entire ranch.

CHAPTER FOUR

Fire? Sylvie was instantly wide awake, fear cascading over her. She threw on a sweatshirt over her sleep shirt and pulled on jeans. After thrusting her feet into her boots, she ran outside. Billows of smoke were coming from the far corner of the barn, but she noticed the horses were all out in the corral.

What in the world?

Dawson had found the long garden hose and turned it on. He pulled it toward the barn, but it probably wouldn't make it the entire distance. She knew there was another hose inside the barn, they used it for cleaning stalls, so she let him take the outside while she went in.

The smoke was thick and heavy. She started to cough and pulled up the edge of her sweatshirt to cover her nose and mouth as she found the water spigot. Her eyes watered and burned, but she cranked the water on high and began spraying the walls of the barn.

Doing so only created more smoke, but she didn't care. Her goal wasn't just to save the barn structure but to prevent the fire from spreading. Wildfires were dangerous, and while June wasn't the driest month of the year, they hadn't seen a ton of rain either.

The seriousness of the situation had her murmuring a desperate prayer.

Lord, please help us control this fire!

Soon other ranch hands came running to help.

"Check the horses," she said, her voice ragged from smoke. Several spun away to do that.

She was grateful for the additional hands, but she didn't relinquish the hose, continuing to spray water over every surface while slowly moving deeper into the barn. Her efforts combined with Dawson's seemed to be working. The smoke thinned, revealing blackened wood.

But no flames.

Not trusting her smoke-blurred eyes, she continued soaking the barn with water. As upset as she was with the fire, she couldn't help feeling relieved the animals were outside.

Logically, she knew that meant the fire had been set on purpose but with no intention of hurting the livestock.

Harming the horses would lower the value of the property.

"Sylvie? Where are you?" Dawson's voice was rough too.

"Here." Her voice was worse, barely loud enough to be heard. A fit of coughing hit hard as she lowered the hose and examined the interior of the barn.

The fire was out, leaving charred wood and a large hole in the wall. It took her a moment to realize there had been a stack of hay piled there earlier. It was gone now, burned to a crisp. Clearly, it had been used to start the fire.

"Sylvie!" Dawson's voice was louder now, and she

turned to find him coming up behind her. "Come on, we need to get out of here."

It took her a moment to realize the ceiling of the barn was also charred black from the fire. Understanding the entire structure was unstable, she allowed Dawson to tug her away. She stopped just long enough to shut off the water spigot, tossing the hose into the equipment room and then heading out into blessedly clear mountain air.

Still, she couldn't seem to stop coughing. Dawson was coughing too, but not as badly as she was. Kilo was running back and forth, obviously concerned about the fire and the horses. Dawson pulled her far away from the barn where the breeze could wash over them.

After several long minutes, she was able to breathe without feeling like she was swallowing razor blades. She dragged her gaze up to meet Dawson's. "That fire was set on purpose."

"I know. The damage was only to the structure, not to the livestock." Dawson pulled her into his arms for a tight hug. "This is serious, Sylvie. If Kilo hadn't started growling and wanting to go out, I wouldn't have seen it in time. The fire could have spread through the entire ranch."

"I know." She leaned on his strength for a long moment before pulling away to rake her gaze over the damaged barn. Ranch hands swarmed the area, muttering among themselves. She had no idea if one of them was responsible or if the fire had been started by Sean, Paul, or even Josh.

She didn't want to believe any of them would do this to her, but the evidence was glaringly obvious that someone had.

"We'll need to work on repairs come morning," she said. "At least it's June and not the middle of winter. The horses will be okay outside for a few days."

"Sylvie?" Josh crossed over to join them, his brow creased in a frown. "What happened?"

"You tell me." She didn't bother to hide the edge in her tone. "You're the foreman, how did this happen under your watch?"

His eyes widened in shock, and he actually took a step back as if she'd slugged him in the gut. "I don't know. It's the middle of the night, anyone could have done this."

"Are all the ranch hands accounted for?" Dawson asked.

Josh swung to look at him. "Two guys, Eddie and Calvin, left yesterday to visit their respective families. But everyone else was in the bunkhouse when we woke to the scent of smoke."

"The livestock were put in the corral before the fire was set." She drilled him with a steely gaze. "Whoever did this didn't want to injure the animals."

"I thought maybe you got the horses out," Josh admitted.

"No, the arsonist did that," Dawson drawled. "Pretty nice of him to make sure the horses were okay, don't you think?"

Josh flushed at the veiled accusation. "Look, I didn't have anything to do with this. I smelled smoke, woke up, and came outside to see you two fighting the fire. Why would I try to take down the barn? Repairing the building makes more work for me."

"For all of us," Sylvie corrected. "Get the horses separated into different paddocks for the rest of the night."

"Sure thing." Josh's tone was subdued as he turned away. She had no idea if Josh was telling her the truth or not. At this point, she didn't trust anyone.

Except Dawson.

For a nanosecond, she considered the possibility that Dawson had started the fire, then had come inside to wake her up. Then she shook off the thought.

Dawson had risked his life to fight the fire. He'd been with her on lizard trail when the boulder came down and had shoved her out of the way, and he had deflected the pitchfork that had come flying toward her. There was a slim possibility he was working with an accomplice, but her gut said otherwise.

The man had put his life on the line over the years while serving his country as a SEAL. Besides, what was his motive? If she were honest, she would admit that Dawson didn't seem the type to settle down as a rancher. Why else would he have spent twenty years in the navy?

He didn't want her ranch, and she believed him when he said his father didn't want it either.

But someone sure did.

"Sylvie? What's going on?"

She spun toward her father's voice. He stood in the doorway, gaping at the activity taking place yards from the house. Dawson put his arm around her waist and walked with her toward the house to talk to her dad.

"There was a fire in the barn, but it's been taken care of now." She tried to smile reassuringly. "Nothing for you to worry about. None of the horses were inside."

"How did that happen?" Her dad looked bewildered. "Where's Josh?"

She swallowed a sigh. Part of the reason the ranch hands didn't respect her authority might be because her father leaned on Josh rather than on her in times of crisis. He claimed to be retired but then went to Josh with any problems rather than coming to her.

"I told him to take care of separating the horses. He claims he was asleep when the fire started."

"You don't believe him?" her father asked.

"I didn't say that." She glanced at Dawson, trying to silently warn him not to spill the beans on the threats against her. He frowned but gave a small nod of agreement. "Dawson noticed the fire first, then alerted me. Thankfully, we were able to douse the flames before they got out of control."

"Kilo was the one who warned me about the fire," Dawson said. "He growled the minute he smelled smoke. I didn't realize Sylvie had gone inside the barn to use the hose inside the building. If I had known, I'd have switched places with her."

"God was watching over you both," her dad said.

She nodded, then dropped to her knees to hug the lab. "Thank you, Kilo."

"Tell Josh I want to talk to him when he's finished," her father said. "A barn fire is unacceptable."

She rested her forehead on the top of Kilo's broad head for a moment before rising to her feet. "I've already made that clear, Dad. The important thing now is to keep the livestock safe and to repair the barn as soon as possible."

"Sylvie has the situation under control, Connor," Dawson added. "She risked her life to go inside the barn to fight the fire. And she'll talk to the ranch hands, especially if there's a chance one of them carelessly started the blaze."

Her father's gaze softened. "I'm glad you're not hurt, Sylvie." He leaned against the doorjamb, then turned away. "We'll talk more tomorrow."

"Sure." She watched as her father slowly retreated. "Thanks for the vote of confidence," she said to Dawson.

"You deserve recognition for what you did tonight."

Dawson was frowning at the ranch house. "Your father should know you're more than capable of running the ranch."

"He does." Most of the time. She sighed, then added, "I think it's a knee-jerk reaction for him to seek out Josh. They worked together for twenty years." She glanced one more time out at the damaged barn. "We'll need to get started on the repairs ASAP. Tomorrow will be a long day."

"I'll stick around and help," Dawson offered.

"Only if your dad doesn't need you." She said the words, although deep down she wanted nothing more than for Dawson to stay with her. Not just tomorrow but until they'd figured out who had targeted her.

An alarming realization, in more ways than one.

DAWSON WAS TORN between helping his dad and staying to protect Sylvie. He followed her inside, knowing that if he had a choice, he'd stay right here.

But that wasn't fair to his father or Max. He told himself that Sylvie should be safe while working with the ranch hands on rebuilding the barn.

Although the simple truth was that Sylvie wouldn't be safe. Not until they caught the guy responsible.

He considered calling his teammates for help but then decided against it. Dallas was the only one who knew anything about ranching, and last he'd heard, the guy was dealing with his own family issues. Nico was still searching for Ava, and the other guys had all found women to spend their lives with.

There was no doubt one of them would come running if he called, but what could they do? He didn't think they knew how to ride, except maybe for Dallas, and that was a large part of working the ranch.

It would be difficult to keep up with Sylvie without being able to ride a horse.

No, he'd feel better if he was the one keeping her safe. Even if that meant finding help for his dad.

His clothes reeked of smoke. Before he could find a way to ask Sylvie for spare clothes, she showed up in his doorway holding several pairs of jeans, shirts, socks, and boxers. "These are from my dad and Sean, hopefully you'll find something useful."

"Thanks, I appreciate that." He gladly took the clothing. She went into another coughing fit that made him frown. "Are you sure you're okay?"

She waved a hand. "Fine. It will take time for my lungs to recover." She tried to smile. "Good thing I never took up smoking. That should help, right?"

"Right." His gaze dropped to her very kissable mouth. "Uh, thanks again. Good night."

"Good night." She turned away.

"Come, Kilo." He stepped back and pointed to the spot on the floor next to the bed. "Lie down."

Kilo stretched out and rested his head between his paws.

Changing out of his smoky clothes helped, but the stench lingered annoyingly in his nostrils. Dawson managed to get a few hours of sleep before Kilo nudged him.

He pushed himself upright with a groan. In the cold light of day, his abdominal muscles and the rest of his body ached as if he'd run a marathon rather than fight a fire.

Man, he was getting too old for this.

Ignoring the pain, he got up, dressed in the borrowed clothes, and opened his bedroom door. No surprise to see

Sylvie's door was open and there were noises coming from the kitchen.

The woman had more stamina than the Energizer Bunny. Admirable and annoying at the same time.

"Good morning," he said, his voice still raspy from the smoke. "I need to take Kilo out."

"That's fine, coffee will be ready by then." Her voice was worse than his, and he wished she'd consider getting checked out at the local clinic. Unfortunately, the town was a good twenty minutes away, and he doubted she'd agree.

The only bright side was that Chief Deputy Rick Holmes was due to come out this morning to talk about the threats Sylvie had reported. At least the deputy would be able to see the damage for himself.

Would the sheriff's department agree to post a deputy on the ranch for a couple of days? It couldn't hurt to ask.

When he returned to the kitchen, the scent of coffee intermixed with the lingering odor of smoke. He wondered how long it would take to get that smell off him.

Why anyone smoked cigarettes was a mystery. He could barely stand the smell.

"Why don't you let me make breakfast?" He took a few minutes to give Kilo fresh food and water. "I can whip up some eggs for us."

She raised a brow. "First offering to clean up and now offering to cook? I'm impressed."

"It's not a big deal, I have to cook for myself all the time." He gently nudged her out of the way. "Sit down and rest a bit. When do you think Deputy Holmes will show up?"

"I have no idea." She did as he asked, cradling her coffee between her hands. "He'll have to take the threats seriously now."

"He better." Dawson quickly broke eggs into a bowl and whipped them together. He poked his head in the fridge, found plenty of fixings for omelets, and helped himself. "I'll make some for your dad too."

"I'm not an invalid." Connor's voice was terse as he came into the kitchen. The older man moved gingerly toward the table, then slowly lowered himself into a chair. "What's this about the sheriff's department?"

"I thought we should report the fire," Sylvie said quickly. "Just to be on the safe side."

"I'm sure it was a careless accident." Her father scowled. "No need to drag the deputies into our personal business."

"I hope you like omelets," Dawson interrupted, sensing an argument. "When do you expect Rhonda Joseph to be back?"

"She should be here by Monday," Connor replied. "I'm sure Sylvie and I can manage another four days."

"Absolutely," Sylvie agreed. "Although I'll need to come up with something for dinner. The chili will only last another day or two at the most."

Dawson wanted to ask why Connor didn't make dinner but kept his thoughts to himself. Maybe the older man hadn't bothered to learn how to cook. He vaguely remembered his dad mentioning how Sylvie's mother had passed away after suffering a brain aneurysm about fifteen years ago. Living in remote locations could be detrimental to getting access to medical care. He'd heard her mother was gone by the time they'd gotten the chopper fired up for transport.

Still, he was irked that Connor expected Sylvie to run the ranch and to cook.

"There's plenty of meat in the freezer," Connor said. "A pot roast would be nice."

Dawson ground his teeth together, but Sylvie just said, "Good idea, Dad."

The omelets didn't take long. He plated the first two for Sylvie and Connor, then took the last one for himself. He joined them at the table. "I'd like to say grace."

Connor nodded and took Sylvie's hand as he bowed his head. Dawson had to give him credit for that, and he tried to let go of his resentment on Sylvie's behalf.

"Dear Lord, we thank You for this food we are about to eat. We ask that You continue to guide us on Your chosen path. Amen."

"Amen," Connor echoed.

"Amen," Sylvie added.

"Dig in," he joked, remembering how Kaleb had always prayed before they'd eaten MREs, which hardly counted as real food. Then again, having something to eat was better than nothing.

As they ate, he noticed Connor only ate about half his omelet before pushing his plate away. He knew the poor guy probably didn't have his normal appetite back, and he felt guilty for being annoyed with him.

He knew what it was like to feel weak and helpless. Hadn't he taken his bad mood out on the nursing staff? He'd apologized afterward, brought them treats to make up for his less than pleasant behavior. But he knew his peace offering hadn't taken the sting from his words.

More reason to give Connor the benefit of the doubt.

"Thanks for breakfast, Dawson," Sylvie said, breaking the silence. "It's delicious."

"Not a problem." He made a mental note to check out the

freezer when he was finished. He could easily throw a roast in a slow cooker, assuming they had one. He'd noticed there were potatoes and carrots in the fridge that he could add as well.

"Call the deputy and tell him there's no reason to come all the way out here," Connor said. "I'm sure they have better things to do."

"Actually, I think Deputy Holmes should come out to see the damage," Dawson said. Sylvie glared at him, but he pushed on undeterred. "Maybe the fire was the result of someone being careless, but imagine what would have happened if we hadn't gotten it under control. The fire could have taken over half the mountain, maybe even reaching the neighboring ranches. If you ask me, it would be good to have the ranch hands questioned by the police. Maybe the person responsible will think twice before doing something like that again."

"Bah," Connor groused. "The fire is over and done with. Seems like they should be more concerned with real crime."

"How do you know this isn't the work of someone who has struck before?" Dawson pressed. "Maybe one of the ranch hands likes to start fires for fun. We both know the ranch hands often move from ranch to ranch, especially if they stir up trouble. Have you acquired new staff recently?"

Connor considered this. "Sure. You know how things go, some of these guys have itchy feet. They don't all stay in one spot forever. I think we've had four new guys start in the past few months, right, Sylvie?"

"Yes. Tim March, Stuart Acorn, Vance Tippens, and Roland Carver." Dawson was impressed with how easily she rattled off the names.

"See what I mean?" Dawson pinned Connor with a serious look. "What if one of those guys had caused trouble on another ranch? There's no way to know if you have a bad egg if you don't talk to the authorities."

Connor seemed to consider this. "Maybe."

"Dawson's right, Dad." Sylvie patted his hand. "Even if the new guys aren't responsible, I think it's a good idea for Deputy Holmes to put this on record in case something similar happens again."

"More coffee anyone?" Dawson stood and reached for the pot.

"No thanks," Connor said. "I'm fine."

Sylvie nodded and pushed her mug within reach. "Thanks."

"You're welcome." He refilled his and then resumed his seat. He was glad Sylvie had eaten all of her omelet.

"Dad, maybe you should get some rest." Sylvie's gaze was full of concern. "You have another radiation treatment coming up next week, don't you? You need your strength."

"Yeah, yeah." Connor sighed. "Only two more to go. I'll be glad when they're over for good."

"I know, Dad." Sylvie finished her omelet and stood. "Come on, let's get you settled in front of the TV so you can watch your favorite shows."

"Daytime TV sucks," her father announced. "If it wasn't for those streaming services you arranged for me, I'd be bored out of my mind."

"I know, Dad." It sounded to Dawson as if Sylvie and her father had this same conversation often. He finished his meal and his coffee. When Sylvie and Connor left the kitchen, he gathered the plates, filled the sink with soapy water, then explored the freezer.

By the time Sylvie returned, he had dishes washed and rinsed and the roast thawing in warm water. "Hey, the beef roast was a great idea. If you can find a slow cooker, I'll do the rest. It won't take but a few minutes to cut up the potatoes and carrots. I'll take care of it so you don't have to."

"Dawson, I didn't expect you to take over Rhonda's chores," she protested. "That's not your job, it's mine."

Since he still thought Connor could have helped, he shook his head and tried to lighten the mood with a grin. "Hey, one thing the military teaches is teamwork. I was forced to count on my teammates to survive." Then his smile faded. "I wouldn't be here today if not for my buddies looking out for me. Our last mission—suffice it to say, it was the worst extraction we'd ever been through." And Jaydon hadn't made it through at all.

"I can believe it," she said, her tone sober. "I'm sure you faced many dangerous situations."

"A few, but none like what you're experiencing here, Sylvie." He wasn't lying. "We fought the enemy, yes, but that was what I'd signed up for. It's very different when the bad guy is someone close to you."

"Yeah." She looked so lost and forlorn he could barely stand it.

He dried his hands on a dish towel and carefully drew her into his arms. Kilo bumped his head against his thigh, but he ignored the dog. "We're going to get through this, Sylvie, I promise."

After a moment's hesitation, she relaxed into his embrace. "I hope so, Dawson. I don't know how much more of this I can take."

His heart broke for what she was going through. The very idea that her brother or ex-husband could be responsible for hurting her like this made his blood boil.

Sylvie lifted her head from his chest and gazed up at him. This close, he could see the tiny flecks of yellow around her pupils in her green eyes.

Then she shocked the daylights out of him when she lifted up onto her tippy-toes to kiss him. It didn't take but a nanosecond for the sweetness of her lips to fire into his brain. He cradled her close and kissed her back the way he'd wanted from the moment he'd pulled her to safety.

CHAPTER FIVE

Dawson's heated kiss was more than Sylvie had bargained for. Yet she couldn't seem to pull away, despite the warning signals flashing bright red in her head. When Dawson deepened their kiss, she felt herself floating off the ground.

Whoa, what was she doing?

With superhuman willpower, she managed to break off their kiss. Her legs were wobbly, but she did her best to stand on her own two feet. She barely noticed Kilo bumping into her with his head as if wanting to share in the embrace.

Uh, where were they? What were they doing? She gazed around the kitchen as if she'd never seen it before.

"That was incredible," Dawson drawled, a grin spreading across his features. "We should try it again."

Yes. No! She pulled her scattered thoughts together. She'd been married, but Paul hadn't sent her mind spinning the way Dawson did. She cleared her throat. "Ah, no, we shouldn't. I was just—" She couldn't finish because she had no clue what she'd been doing. She never should have kissed him.

"I'm here if you change your mind," Dawson murmured.

"I'm grateful for your support, but I have work to do." She forced herself to take several steps back. "And I'm sure you have to get back to the Copper Creek too."

Mentioning his father's ranch caused his brow to furrow. "Yeah, I need to check in with my dad. But I won't leave you here alone for long."

"I'm fine." She put as much emphasis on the words as she could muster. The horror from the barn fire that she knew full well had been set on purpose lingered in the back of her mind, nagging like a sore tooth. She hoped Deputy Rick Holmes would show up sooner rather than later. Her cough was better, but her throat was still sore. "I need to get out there and check on the horses."

"Go ahead, I'll join you as soon as I can."

She nodded, then turned away. It wasn't until she was outside looking at what was left of the barn that she remembered he was making pot roast. She was torn between going back inside to help—as it wasn't his job to cook for them—and continuing on to check on the horses.

When she saw Josh riding Storm, she narrowed her gaze and immediately crossed over to the corral. This was the second time she'd noticed him riding the stallion as if it were his own. "Hey, how is Storm doing? Is he okay after the fire?"

"He's still a bit jittery," Josh said. "Good thing I found him in his paddock, I was worried he'd go after the mares."

He stopped in front of her, and she held his gaze. "Seems as if whoever started the fire made sure Storm and the other horses were safe."

"I know how this looks, but it wasn't me," Josh said without hesitation. "I wouldn't do something so reckless."

"Not even to convince me to leave?"

"No! Come on, this is your home, Sylvie. Why would I want you to leave?"

Nice words, but she wasn't sure she believed the sentiment behind them. In her mind, Josh was still a suspect. Although what he'd hoped to gain was a mystery. It wasn't like her father would sell him the ranch, even if Josh could afford it, which she knew full well he couldn't.

Scaring her wasn't likely to change anything either. She ducked between the fence rails and strode over to where a group of geldings and mares were huddled together.

"Easy now, it's okay." She stroked Alice, another of her favorite mares, then smiled when Fanny nudged her, wanting her fair share of attention too. Concern for her horses brought tears to her eyes, but she quickly swiped at them before Josh or any of the ranch hands could see. "We are all going to be fine."

There wasn't enough time to do a full nose-to-hoof inspection of every horse, but overall, they seemed unharmed. No signs of burns or other injuries. She'd call the veterinarian and ask him to take a trip out to examine them more closely.

Satisfied for the moment, she headed back over to the charred barn. The damage was mostly focused on the back wall, where the haystack had been. Somehow it looked worse in the daylight, making her angry all over again.

Josh had put Storm back in his paddock and joined her. Several of the ranch hands were milling about too.

"We need to get this repaired ASAP." She swept her gaze over the group. "I want a team of you to pull the damaged wood down, while Josh and Ace head to town to get new lumber."

There was a moment's pause as the ranch hands looked at Josh. She ground her teeth together in frustration.

"You heard the lady. Let's get it done." Josh gestured for Ace Abbott to follow him. "We'll take the Suburban."

Ace nodded, and the rest of the cowboys scattered to get the tools they'd need to get to work. She sighed and eyed the damage again.

As if there wasn't enough work to do on the ranch.

She was about to turn to head back inside to check on Dawson and the pot roast when she noticed a police squad coming down the long, winding driveway. The squad passed Josh and Ace in the Suburban but didn't slow down. A minor point in the deputy's favor that he didn't try to talk to the ranch foreman before meeting with her.

Although she wouldn't have minded the deputy questioning Josh and Ace, along with the others. As she waited for the deputy to arrive, Dawson and Kilo came out of the house to join her.

"I'm sorry I left the cooking for you," she began, but he waved her off.

"It's all set. Glad to see the cops have arrived."

"Me too." When Deputy Holmes came to a stop, she moved forward. "Glad to see you, Rick. We had another incident last night."

"You did?" He looked surprised. "What happened?"

"I'll show you." She turned and strode toward the barn. Holmes, Dawson, and Kilo followed.

Holmes let out a low whistle when he saw the charred boards and hole in the back wall of the barn. "A fire?"

"Set on purpose. All the horses had been removed from the barn, the stallion, Storm, was put in his own paddock to keep him from the other horses." She arched a brow. "Considerate of the arsonist to take care of the livestock, don't you think?"

Holmes pushed the rim of his hat upward as he surveyed the damage. "This is serious, Sylvie. He could have started a wildfire."

"Yes, it's very serious. Especially when you add in the other attempts to hurt me." She was glad Dawson stayed back, allowing her to take the lead. "Three, no wait, four attacks in less than twenty-four hours are not a coincidence."

"Four?" Rick echoed.

She ticked them off her fingers. "Gunshot causing me to be thrown off my horse, boulder sent down the ravine while we were going down lizard trail, the pitchfork that came flying at me in the barn, missing me by inches, and lastly this fire."

Deputy Holmes let out a breath. "Obviously not a coincidence. We'll get them all documented, Sylvie."

She gestured to the hole in the wall. "I believe the source of the fire was here, where it burned the hottest. There were a couple of stacks of hay sitting there, which are nothing but ash now."

"I see that." Deputy Holmes rubbed the edge of his jaw, before swinging around to look at her. "You must have an idea of who is behind these incidents."

"My foreman, Josh O'Leary, my ex-husband, Paul Griffin, my brother, Sean McLane." She shrugged. "Possibly Max Wolfe, foreman from the Copper Creek Ranch."

Dawson moved forward as if to protest, but she narrowed her gaze in warning, so he kept his mouth shut. These were her list of suspects, not his.

And she wasn't about to pull any punches.

"What about you?" Deputy Holmes turned to Dawson.

"I would never hurt Sylvie, but I understand why you would consider me a suspect. However, I pulled Sylvie to safety, was with her when the boulder came crashing down, and was standing beside her when the pitchfork came flying toward us. Kilo here"—he gestured to his yellow lab— "alerted us to the fire. If he hadn't growled in warning, the blaze may have spread to other buildings and the rest of the ranch."

"Okay, that leaves four suspects," Deputy Holmes said with a nod. "I'll need to talk to them and to the others."

"Any chance we can get a deputy here to keep an eye on things?" Dawson asked.

Rick shook his head. "Sorry, we're not staffed for that."

"It's fine. Josh and Ace just left to get lumber," Sylvie told him. "But I would appreciate you starting with the ranch hands who are here now. Any of them could have been hired to do one or more of these attacks."

"Will do." Holmes nodded and moved over to the group of guys who lingered nearby. Sylvie wanted to listen to hear what they had to say, but there was too much work to be done.

She had to haul hay out to feed the horses, then help work on the barn repairs. She turned away, but Dawson caught her arm.

"Listen, I told my dad I need to stick around here for a while, so put me to work. What do you want me to do?"

"Are you sure? I feel bad keeping you from helping your dad."

"He assured me Max has everything under control." Dawson hesitated, then said, "I really don't think the Copper Creek foreman is involved."

"Maybe not." She couldn't help but sigh. "But think about it, Dawson. We're looking at anyone who might have a reason to scare me off. It's not a secret that your dad has first dibs on the ranch if my dad decides to sell. Max knows that, as do all the ranch hands. That kind of news gets around mighty quick."

"Yeah, but Max doesn't have the money to buy out my dad, much less this ranch. And frankly, neither does Josh."

"That doesn't mean they aren't looking for a shortcut to owning property of their own. And face it, your dad and mine would likely set up in a will for either of our foremen to inherit the ranch if you and I were both out of the picture. It's not as if either one of us has extended family to take over."

"Except in your case, the ranch would go to your brother first."

"Right." She couldn't argue. Deep in her heart she knew the two most logical suspects were her ex-husband and her brother.

Two men who had once been so close to her but who were now apparently willing to ruthlessly stab her in the back, or worse.

Doing whatever was necessary to get what they wanted.

THE PAIN in Sylvie's green gaze gnawed at him. He hated how vulnerable she was here. Impossible to find one man, or even two, hiding somewhere within the fifteen hundred acres that comprised McLane Mountain Ranch.

His plan was to stick to her like glue, but he really needed to get back to the Copper Creek. For one thing, he needed more dog food and other supplies for Kilo. Additional clothes for himself, ones that weren't borrowed and didn't reek like smoke, would be nice too. But a big part of leaving was so that he could check on his dad.

"Rick seems to be taking this seriously," Sylvie said, looking over to where the deputy had pulled one of the ranch hands aside to talk to him out of earshot of the others. "That's a good sign."

"It is, yes. I need to head back to the Copper Creek, Sylvie." He rested his hand on her arm. "I'd like you to stick around the group of ranch hands while I'm gone, don't go off anywhere alone. I'll return as quickly as possible."

"I understand, and I'll be fine." Her smile was forced, and he knew she was anything but fine.

Maybe he could get back before the deputy finished up. He strode toward the corral where Diamond was waiting. He detoured into the barn to grab his tack, then went out to saddle his horse.

"Come, Kilo." He figured the dog should be able to keep up while he took the most direct route to his dad's place. It wasn't scenic, but speed and efficiency were more important.

Kilo loved to run and easily kept up. But when the canine grew tired, he slowed Diamond's pace. "You okay, boy?"

Kilo looked up at him and wagged his tail.

Dawson swept a keen gaze over the area, searching for signs of anything unusual. But he didn't see anything on the trip back to the Copper Creek. He headed straight for the barn, expecting to see Max Wolfe, but there was no sign of the foreman.

Because he was hiding somewhere on McLane Mountain? He didn't really believe Max to be a serious suspect.

After caring for Diamond, he headed up to the house with Kilo at his side. He'd already decided to drive his SUV back to Sylvie's place. She had plenty of horses he could borrow if needed, and he already had most of Kilo's stuff stored in his SUV.

"Dad?" Dawson frowned when there was no answer to his call. A niggle of worry ate at him as he checked the living room, then headed to his father's master bedroom.

Both were empty. His Dad's truck was parked next to his SUV, so he hadn't left the ranch that way.

Was his dad riding so soon? He knew the physical therapists had cautioned his dad to take it slow.

Dawson hurried outside again, Kilo shadowing him. In the distance, he could see two riders making their way back from the east pasture. It wasn't easy to see their features, but he felt certain the two riders were Max and his dad.

He packed his clothes in a large duffel and took it outside to his SUV. Then he stored Kilo's fifty-pound bag of dog food next to it. He idly rubbed his abdominal muscles that were still achy after rescuing Sylvie and fighting the fire last night.

"Dawg? Is that you?"

Dawson tried not to grimace as Max used his old SEAL nickname. For some reason, it bugged him that the ranch foreman who hadn't served in the military thought he could call him by the name his SEAL teammates used. Max learned about the nickname when his buddy had called asking for Dawg. Max wasn't his best friend, but maybe he was letting Sylvie's suspicions mess with his head.

"Hey, good to see you both. Dad, I'm surprised you're riding again. That therapist told you to take it easy, didn't he?"

"Bah"—his father waved a hand—"been riding my whole life, not going to give it up now."

Dawson sighed and decided there was no point in arguing, especially since there was no sign of discomfort on his dad's face. Landon Steele clearly wasn't going to give up riding unless the pain got to him.

"Heard there was trouble last night at the Double M," Max said.

Many of the locals called McLane Mountain the Double M, although that was not the name of the ranch. He kept his gaze on Max. "What did you hear?"

"There was a fire in the barn." Max looked at him with a frown. "We could smell the smoke all the way out here. I sent a ranch hand to investigate in case we had a wildfire brewing."

The foreman's explanation made sense, so Dawson nodded. "Yeah, there was a fire. Thankfully, we were able to douse the flames before they spread."

"I can't believe someone was so careless as to start a fire," his dad said. When his old man dismounted from his horse, a flicker of discomfort flashed across his features. "That could have ended very badly."

He eyed the two men for a long moment, debating how much to tell them. Then he realized that the truth would get out soon once Sylvie's ranch hands were finished being questioned by the deputy.

"The fire was started on purpose." He watched Max's expression carefully. "The arsonist was thoughtful enough to take all the horses out of the barn, putting them in various paddocks, including isolating their stallion."

"What? Who would do that?" his father demanded.

Dawson didn't look away from Max. "Did you hear anything about that, Max?"

There was a moment's hesitation before the foreman nodded. "Yeah, you know how these cowboys talk. They gossip worse than a church full of old ladies."

Maybe, Dawson thought. Or maybe Max knew more because he was involved in some way.

"That still doesn't make any sense," his father said with a frown. "What's the point of scaring Sylvie? What do they hope to gain?"

Dawson didn't reply, again watching Max. The foreman swung down from his mount. "Rumor has it the fire was an attempt to pressure Sylvie into selling the place."

"What?" His father looked horrified by that. "That's nuts! Sylvie has been doing a great job running the place while Connor is being treated for cancer."

"Hey, I'm just repeating what some of the guys are saying." Max turned to face Dawson. "What does Connor think?"

"Deputy Holmes is at McLane Mountain now, questioning everyone about the fire." Dawson didn't answer Max's question. "I'm wondering if I should have Holmes come here, too, to talk to your guys since they seem to be a wealth of information."

A spark of anger darkened Max's gaze. "That's not necessary, no one here is responsible for anything that took place at the Double M last night."

Dawson wished he could believe him. "I'll leave that decision up to the deputy." Then he turned toward his dad. "I'm planning to head back over to Sylvie's for a couple of days, if that's okay with you."

"Sure, sure. I'm fine." Seeing his father riding was somewhat reassuring. "Max has everything under control."

"I'm glad to hear it." Dawson wasn't lying, he truly was glad his dad had Max's help. "Thanks, Max. I appreciate everything you're doing here."

"It's my job." Max's tone was curt, and he scowled as he

reached for the reins of his dad's horse. "I'll take care of these rides and check in later."

Dawson watched him leave, then took his dad's arm to go inside. "I hope you didn't overdo the horseback riding."

"We took a short ride to the east pasture and back. The cattle are looking good, and Max is planning to move half the herd to the south pasture later today." His dad eased himself into a kitchen chair. "I'm troubled by the fire."

"Me too. Which is why I'm heading over there for a few days." He hesitated, then asked, "Dad, if I decided not to stay in Montana, would you gift the ranch to Max?"

His father frowned. "I'd rather you take over the ranch, Dawson."

"I know, but if I didn't want to, what would you do? Max often acts as if he's a co-owner of the place."

"That's only because he's lived here for the past twenty-five years. But if you're asking me if I'd sell Max the ranch if you didn't want it? I can't do that, the right of first refusal goes to Connor and Sylvie. If they turned it down, then I'd consider Max. Although I'd like you to agree to the terms."

"I don't need your money, Dad. I've done fine for myself over the years."

"My dad took over from his dad after settling here nearly ninety years ago." His father's expression was serious. "I'm not going to lie, Dawson. It would hurt me to sell the property to someone else. I was hoping you'd settle down here, maybe raise a family of your own."

Sylvie's face, flushed from his kiss, flashed in his mind. "I understand, Dad. I'll see how things work out. For now, I need to protect Sylvie. I hope you can understand that."

"Sure thing. I've always liked that gal." The suggestive look in his father's eye made it clear his old man would love nothing more than the two ranches to be merged by his marrying Sylvie.

Too bad, Dawson wasn't necessarily sure he wanted to be a rancher. Just thinking about being stuck in one place for the rest of his life brought a sense of dread.

No way. Uh-uh. He couldn't imagine it.

"Okay, I'll check in with you later, Dad. Come, Kilo." He strode to the door, glancing back at his father one more time. He could tell his dad was trying to figure out where he went wrong with raising Dawson. Why his own son wasn't interested in his legacy.

Times like this, he wished he had brothers. It was a heavy burden to know he was disappointing his father.

He opened the back of the SUV for Kilo. Once the dog was settled, he slid in behind the wheel and took the driveway to the narrow ribbon of highway. The driving route to Sylvie's was longer than riding across the open fields, giving him way too much time with his troubled thoughts.

It wasn't fair to flirt with Sylvie if he wasn't planning on sticking around for the long term. She'd already been through one divorce and was struggling to keep the ranch going in the face of adversity. She didn't need him piling on more trouble.

His primary goal was to keep her safe. He wasn't looking for a wife or a life partner, certainly not someone with roots dug deep into the relentless Montana soil. Which meant no more cuddling, kissing, or generally enjoying her company.

A task easier said than done.

Soon, he pulled up in front of Sylvie's ranch house. To his dismay, there was no sign of the sheriff's deputy squad car. He hadn't passed it along the road, so the deputy must have left a while ago.

Not a good investigative job in his opinion.

He let Kilo out, and then glanced around for Sylvie. There were several ranch hands working on the horse barn, so he headed in that direction. Then frowned when he noticed the guy on top of the barn roof wasn't a man at all.

It was Sylvie. He inwardly groaned, knowing he should have figured she'd be the one up top ready and willing to prove herself as capable as any of the other guys.

"Sylvie?" he called out as he approached. She looked up from her work, halting the process of removing a singed board.

"What?" She sounded a bit cranky.

"Come on down, I'd like to talk to you for a few minutes." He wanted to update her on the conversation he had with Max Wolfe but not in front of an audience.

She hesitated, then nodded in agreement. She finished removing the board she'd been working on, tossing it to the ground, then moved toward the edge of the roof. A tall ladder was propped along the side.

But before she made it to the edge, the boards beneath her feet creaked loudly. Dawson could tell what was going to happen seconds before she let out a cry as her feet broke through the roof. Dawson darted through the hole along the back of the barn in time to grab her legs to prevent her from falling the rest of the way.

"I've got you." He ignored the pull of his injured abdominal muscles as he lowered her to the concrete floor.

His earlier lecture to himself vanished in the wake of the near disaster. He pulled her in for a tight hug. "Are you okay?"

"I think so." Her voice was muffled against his chest.

Then she pushed away to look up at the roof. "I don't understand what happened. I'd been up there for twenty minutes without a problem."

He followed her gaze, then frowned when he saw a hole in one of the cross beams where a screw should have been. He stepped back, then found the screw on the floor, along with several others. They'd been loosened, and likely not from the fire.

This was yet another act of vandalism.

How many more of these attempts would take place before Sylvie suffered a catastrophic injury?

CHAPTER SIX

For the second time that day, Sylvie found herself in Dawson's arms. Yet seeing the screws lying on the floor and the hole in the ceiling where she'd been standing robbed her of feeling any enjoyment in their embrace.

How many times would she be targeted? Until she was severely injured?

Dead?

"Stay off the roof," Dawson said. "Let the ranch hands take care of it."

"My barn, my job." The words were automatic, although she could see the wisdom in his suggestion. "Yeah, fine, I'll stay off the roof. For now."

"Did you notice anyone hanging around the barn?"

"No one in particular." She culled through her scattered thoughts. "Truthfully, I was focused on getting the work done. But most of the ranch hands have been helping."

"Josh and Ace too?"

She nodded. "They just got back about fifteen minutes ago." Anything was possible, but she thought the time frame was too narrow for the person to have loosened the board to be Josh. Maybe she was wrong about the ranch foreman. What did he gain by her selling the ranch? Nothing.

Unless her brother had somehow convinced him to do the dirty work with the promise of getting a chunk of the inheritance.

"Okay, I'll take over working on the barn," Dawson said firmly. "No one is going up on the roof now anyway. Why don't you go ahead and take care of the horses?"

"I'll call Doc Ernie Dunn, I wanted him to check the herd out anyway." It wasn't easy to step away from the barn repairs, but her knees still felt a little shaky. "Then I'll come back to help."

Dawson rolled his eyes, clearly irritated with her stubbornness, but he didn't say anything else. She handed him the claw hammer she'd been using to pry up the damaged boards, took a moment to pat Kilo on the head, then turned to jump through the burned-out hole in the wall.

Pulling her phone from her pocket, she called the doc. Ernie Dunn was younger than his name would lead a person to believe, he'd been named after his father, so he was technically Ernie Junior. The large animal vet was very good at his job, though, having learned at his father's knee. She trusted his opinion when it came to her livestock.

She scowled, noting her fingers were shaking as she gripped the phone.

"Sylvie? What's going on?"

"Hey, Doc, do you have time to check my horses? There was a barn fire last night. They were out in the corral, but I'd still like you to check them over."

"A fire?" His voice rose in alarm. "How did that happen?"

"Long story." She figured the grapevine would be

vibrating with news before the end of the day. "Are you tied up with something else?"

"Nah, I'm open. I'll be there in an hour."

"Thanks, see you then." She disconnected from the call and turned back to look at the disaster that was her horse barn. Keeping the horses outside all night in the summer wasn't that big of a deal, yet she still didn't like it. Wildlife often wandered around the mountains, and big cats and wolves were known to attack large animals. More so in winter when meat was scarce, but still, it made her nervous. Her goal of having the roof repaired before sundown suddenly seemed far too lofty.

She walked over to the hose and took a drink of water to soothe her raw throat. The water helped cool her throat that still felt as if she'd smoked an entire carton of cigarettes in one sitting.

Not that she'd ever smoked.

Dawson stood near the top of the ladder to remove more boards. She moved around the barn, eyeing which ranch hands were doing various other odd jobs. They were focused on the task at hand, no one looked at her twice.

It was a strange feeling to be standing on your own property, knowing someone close to you had tried to hurt you. Not just once but over and over again.

Drawing in a deep breath, she shook off the despair and headed back over to the damaged wall of the barn. She found another hammer and went to work pulling down charred boards.

Keeping busy was the only way she knew how to cope. And maybe, just maybe, they could get enough work done on the barn today that she could use it as a shelter.

Her arms were tired and sore by the time Doc Ernie

showed up. She gratefully tossed her hammer down and led the vet over to the corral.

"I looked them over for obvious signs of burns but didn't find anything." She glanced at the vet. "Yet they were close enough that they likely inhaled some smoke."

"Sounds like you did too," Doc Ernie said with a frown. "You should be examined by a people doc. You're probably suffering from smoke inhalation, they often treat that with oxygen."

"I'm fine." She wasn't going to waste time driving all the way into town for a sore throat and nagging cough. "The horses are more important."

"Spoken like a true rancher," Doc Ernie teased. Then his expression turned serious. "Go on, Sylvie, this will take me a while."

She nodded and left him to it. Her entire body was sore, but she ignored the pain and went back to work on the barn. An hour later, the entire roof and back wall had been removed.

"Looks like the other walls are intact and stable," Josh said, swiping his face with a bandanna. "You want us to start building the new wall?"

"Give me a minute." She gestured for Dawson to follow her inside the barn. Kilo dogged his heels. "What do you think, Dawson? Should we tear these down too?"

Dawson frowned and began to examine the walls for himself. She knew how to do rough construction, a necessity on a ranch, but gauging the stability of the structure was a bit beyond her.

"I'm no expert, Sylvie, but I don't see any signs of damage." Dawson shrugged. "I'd say trust Josh on this. After all, whoever did this made sure the horses were safe. I doubt he'd put them in danger here."

"Okay, thanks." It helped to hear his opinion. She turned and headed back over to where Josh waited. "Yes, let's start the new wall. When that's finished, we'll work on the roof."

"Got it." If her foreman was annoyed that she'd chosen to listen to Dawson over him, he didn't show it. "I'd like to give the guys a break for lunch."

"Of course." Her own stomach was rumbling with hunger too. "We got farther on this than I dared to hope. We might be able to use it tonight."

"That's the goal." Josh gave her a nod, then turned away to talk to the ranch hands. She eyed Dawson. "Let's head inside and find something to eat."

"Leftover chili and cornbread?" he asked, his blue eyes twinkling with hope.

"You're such a goofball." A reluctant smile tugged at the corner of her mouth. "Sure, why not? We're obviously having roast beef for dinner."

"Can't wait." Dawson and Kilo followed her to the ranch house. As she opened the door, she glanced over her shoulder in time to catch Josh watching them with a scowl etched on his features.

As earlier, Dawson prayed before their meal. She found herself remembering how she'd prayed while fighting the barn fire. Something she hadn't done since her mother died.

"Seems like Deputy Holmes wasn't here very long." Dawson eyed her over his glass of iced tea. "He couldn't possibly have spoken to all the ranch hands in the time I was gone."

"He did his best, but every ranch hand said the same thing, I was sleeping and woke to the fire." She grimaced. "I think he gave up, knowing he wasn't going to get any more information out of them."

"Maybe I need to have a talk with them."

"Why, because you're a man?" She narrowed her gaze. "You're not in charge, Dawson. Just stay out of it."

They ate in silence for several minutes. "Max Wolfe mentioned the fire, claims he sent some ranch hands over to make sure the fire wasn't a danger to the Copper Creek."

The news was interesting but not a total surprise. She managed a wry smile. "I'm sure Josh would have done the same if the situation was reversed. An out-of-control wildfire is a serious threat to all ranchers in the immediate area."

"You're probably right. It just seemed strange to me, that's all." Dawson ate more of his chili.

"You haven't been living the ranch life for the past twenty years, right?"

"True." He stared down at his meal for a moment, then met her gaze. "If I was the one being targeted, I'd suspect Max of being the guy responsible. If I decided not to take over running my father's ranch, I'm pretty sure dad would name Max as his heir."

She nodded slowly. "I can imagine that's true, but I've been here my entire life. There's never been any talk of me giving up the ranch. Quite the opposite. My dad clearly wants me and my brother to run it equally, but Sean isn't on board with that plan."

"I found your brother on social media with a couple of guys." Dawson looked thoughtful for a moment. "Do you know Matt Keagan and/or Ned Burns?"

"Yeah, they're both rodeo friends of Sean's." The chili sat like a lump in her gut. "Why do you ask?"

"You mentioned Sean was staying with a friend, most likely one of those two, right?" Dawson shrugged. "Might be worth checking them out."

"No time today, we have to finish the barn." She hesitated, then added, "If you're still willing to help. If not, that's okay. I know you have other things to do."

"Nothing more important than making sure you're safe."

His declaration warmed her heart. Since her divorce, she felt as if she were fighting to run the ranch all by herself. Sure, Josh and the other ranch hands were there to help, but the decisions were hers. The trials, tribulations, all hers.

She'd protected her father from any and all problems so that he could focus on his health.

Now, for the first time in a long while, she didn't feel completely alone. Dawson was someone she could depend on.

A rare gift, yet also a temporary one.

Because she knew, deep down, Dawson wasn't staying in Montana for long. Once they figured out who was attacking her, she was sure he'd go back. And not to his father's ranch.

No, she didn't think ranching was in Dawson's blood the way it was in hers.

Humbling to realize how much she'd miss him when he left for good.

THE FATIGUE ETCHED in Sylvie's features was concerning. It was only noon, yet she looked as if she'd put in a ten-hour day already. He hated how she was working herself to the bone just to prove she was as capable as Josh and the other ranch hands.

Running a ranch wasn't all brawn and strength, it took smarts. Intelligence he knew Sylvie had, except for the way she'd spent her time pretending to be one of the guys.

He hated to admit it, but his own strength was failing him. His abdominal muscles were extremely sore from the events yesterday and the physical labor he'd done so far today. They both needed a break.

But how to convince her?

"Sylvie, I really think we need to confront your brother. Today. You have a dozen men outside working on the barn. But if we don't get to the bottom of this, which part of the ranch will be targeted next?"

She frowned. "I know, but I need to help."

"Sylvie, listen to me. You're the boss, and a good leader knows how to delegate." He hesitated, then added, "I can't lie, my abdominal muscles are killing me. I'm not sure I can do much more today."

"Oh, of course you shouldn't." A flash of guilt darkened her green eyes. "You've been very helpful."

"Delegate the rest of the work to Josh and his men while we take a ride into town to visit your brother," he repeated. "It's important."

She stared at him for a full minute before reluctantly nodding. "Okay. We'll take a ride to see Sean. Although I don't think he's going to confess."

"No, but he should know that he's a suspect. Maybe he'll back off or give up the fight altogether."

"Doubtful." She pulled her phone from her back pocket. "I'll try calling him again, although he hasn't answered since he left."

"Good idea." He finished his meal while she set the phone on the table. Through the speaker, he could hear ringing, then the automatic voice mail system.

"See?" She stabbed the end button. "Told you. He hasn't spoken to me since I cut him off financially."

Yeah, and that alone provided motivation for him to

come after Sylvie at the ranch. He could all too easily imagine the guy causing the multiple incidents. "All the more reason to talk to him directly."

"Fine. We'll go." She stood and carried her dishes to the sink.

He did the same, gently elbowing her aside. "Go talk to Josh about the barn and check in with your vet. I'll wash these."

She didn't argue. Kilo stretched out on the floor behind him, watching him with wide brown eyes as he worked.

When he finished, he led Kilo back outside. He stood and watched Josh and the others return from the bunkhouse to continue working on the barn. Dawson was confident they'd get the roof built before the end of the day.

It took another ten minutes before he saw Sylvie walking toward the house with the vet. He wasn't close enough to hear their conversation, but he didn't see any sign of bad news on either of their faces.

"Thanks again, Doc." Sylvie shook his hand. "I appreciate you making the time to check the herd."

"No problem." The young vet eyed the barn where the ranch hands were starting to work. "I hope you don't have any more trouble, Sylvie."

"Me too."

Dawson went over to join Sylvie as the doc slid in behind the wheel of his truck and left. He gestured to his SUV. "Better if I drive, Kilo has a crate area in the back."

"Okay, but where exactly are we going?"

"I figure once we get to Dillon, we can ask around for Sean and the other guys, Matt Keagan and Ned Burns." He grinned as he opened the back hatch for Kilo. The yellow lab nimbly jumped inside. "You know how people love to talk. I'm sure we'll find them without a problem."

The corner of her mouth tipped up in a smile. "I know, it's crazy how much everyone knows about everyone else's business. I think the news of my divorce went through the place like wildfire. I find it amazing, considering we live so far outside of town."

After they were settled in the front seat, he started the car and shifted into gear. He headed down the long, winding driveway that would take them to the highway. He glanced at her. "It only takes one person to start talking, and cell phones make that super easy."

"When they work," she argued. "Honestly, mine rarely works anywhere except in Dillon and at the house."

"Phones didn't work most of the time when I was deployed overseas either." He shook off thoughts of his last op and quickly changed the subject. "Any idea where Sean might be working?"

"Other than the rodeo circuit?" She shook her head. "I have no idea."

"We'll find him."

"I hope so." She didn't sound convinced.

"By the way, who works on your chopper?" He'd almost suggested taking the chopper into town, then remembered she'd mentioned it needing a new fuel gauge.

"Sean used to do the majority of the work, but I can do minor repairs too." Her expression brightened. "Hey, I can pick up a new fuel gauge when we get to Dillon. Makes the trip even more worthwhile."

"Glad to help out." He wryly shook his head, wondering when she'd done something just for fun. If the situation wasn't so serious, he'd encourage her to go to dinner and a movie with him. Their explosive kiss seemed to have happened days ago rather than hours.

Yet he'd promised himself not to lead her on.

That meant no dinner and no movie. He needed to stay focused on finding Sean.

The ride to Dillon took a solid twenty minutes. He slowed the SUV as they entered the outskirts of town. "Do you want to pick up the gauge first?"

"Yes, please." She gestured with her hand. "The small engine supply store is over there."

He pulled up in front of the building. She was out of the SUV and striding inside before he had time to shut down the car. He took a moment to pull his Sig Sauer from the glove box, sliding the holster onto his belt, before heading around back to let Kilo out. Because they were in town, he reluctantly put the dog on leash.

"Behave," he told the canine.

Kilo wagged his tail looking all innocent, as if he'd never misbehaved. Dawson wasn't fooled. The dog loved people and seemed to believe they would all love him the same way. Kilo didn't have any boundaries.

Not as much of a watchdog as he'd have liked, although Kilo had growled about the smoke, so maybe he wasn't giving the lab enough credit.

He looked around, curious about where they should start searching for Sean. The guy was only three years younger than Sylvie, yet often acted much younger.

"Got it!" Sylvie lifted the fuel gauge with a wide grin. He could honestly say he'd never met a woman who'd shown this much excitement over a replacement part for a chopper. "Glad you brought it up or I might have forgotten."

She tucked the box in the back seat, then frowned. "You're carrying?"

"Yeah."

She considered this for a moment, then nodded. "I

guess you're not the only one, this is the Wild West after all." She glanced around. "Where do you want to start?"

"The Rocking Wrangler." Her eyes widened when he mentioned the most popular bar in Dillon. "Even if he's not there, chances are good someone hanging out there will know where to find him. And it's centrally located, so we can park there and walk up and down Main Street, too, if need be."

A tiny frown furrowed her brow, but she slowly nodded. "Okay, let's go."

He put Kilo in the back again. Less than five minutes later, he pulled into the very crowded parking lot of the Rocking Wrangler.

"It's Thursday, right?" Sylvie asked. "Why on earth is it so crowded?"

"Summer tourists maybe?" He honestly had no idea if Dillon was a draw for tourism or not. He pushed out of the car and went around back. Taking Kilo inside might be against the rules, but he couldn't leave the dog outside unattended either.

"Not sure dogs are allowed." Sylvie voiced his thoughts.

"We'll see. If they raise a stink, then you can take him outside while I ask around."

"Why me? He's your dog."

"No reason to get all prickly." He was growing weary of her attitude. "I'm assuming if Sean hears about a woman asking around for him, he'll assume it's you, right? So I need to ask about where he is. Therefore if one of us needs to stay outside, it should be you."

"I guess."

The inside wasn't as packed as he'd expected. No one said anything about Kilo, maybe because the canine didn't bark or draw attention. For once the dog stayed close to his side, although his tail wagged back and forth with enough force to be a deadly weapon.

"Do you see Sean?" he asked in a low voice.

Sylvie shook her head. "Not yet."

He took his time, focusing on the faces of the patrons as he searched for Sean or his rodeo buddies. He was blessed with a very good memory, so he could easily recall the faces he'd seen on social media.

But none of the three men were inside the bar. At least, not yet. It's possible they'd stop in later.

"He's not here." Sylvie's tone was dejected.

"Can I help you?" A pretty woman came over holding two menus. She frowned when she saw Kilo. "I'm sorry, dogs aren't allowed."

It was somewhat comical that guns were okay but dogs weren't.

"I'll take him outside." Sylvie took Kilo's leash from his hand. "Come on, Kilo. You're a good boy, aren't you? Yes, you are."

Kilo didn't want to go, but Sylvie managed to get him to obey. Dawson eyed the woman. "Have you seen Sean McLane lately? We're supposed to be meeting him here."

"Not lately, no." She tapped the side of the plastic menu against the palm of her hand. "I think it's been about a week since he was in here with his buddies."

"Matt Keagan and Ned Burns, right?" He smiled broadly. "The three of them hang out a lot from what I hear."

She shrugged. "Ned, Matt, and Sean used to be regulars. Now that you mention it, it's very strange none of them has been in lately."

"Do you know where Sean or the others have been staying?" Dawson gave her a look of concern. "We should check on him, maybe he's been sick or hurt in some way."

"No clue, but a bunch of the rodeo guys stay at the Timber Inn when they're in town." She stopped tapping the menu. "Is Sean in some sort of trouble?"

He arched a brow. "What makes you say that?"

"Nothing." She quickly turned and hurried away.

He swept one more glance over the restaurant, then went out to meet up with Sylvie and Kilo. "Are you familiar with the Timber Inn?"

"No, should I be?"

"The hostess mentioned it as a place where many of the rodeo guys hang out. Can't hurt to swing by." He grinned. "We'll stop for ice cream on the way."

"Ice cream?" She looked at him as if he'd spouted horns. "This isn't a social outing, Steele."

"You have something against ice cream?" Oddly, he was beginning to like it when she went all prickly pear on him. Obviously, it was a sign he was getting under her skin. Not that he'd necessarily tried to do that on purpose.

"No, but I'm still full from lunch, and we're here to find Sean, not eat sweets." She thrust Kilo's leash back into his hand. "Come on, let's go. If I remember correctly, the Timber Inn is on the other end of Main Street."

Oh yeah, it's been a long time since she'd done anything for fun. And that made him sad. He and his SEAL teammates had gone through many dicey situations, but they'd always took time off to have fun.

At least until their last op had gone upside down. Losing Jaydon had been hard, yet that only proved that life was short.

Too short to give up the opportunity to have ice cream on a warm summer day.

He was about to head down Main Street, grimacing a bit when he saw the long line in front of the ice-cream shop, when the sharp report of gunfire rang out.

"Get down!" He yanked Sylvie to the ground as Kilo growled low in his throat. He pulled his Sig Sauer and raked his gaze over the area as people scattered from the sidewalks and streets.

There was no sign of the gunman, but he wasn't taking any chances either. "Get behind the car," he whispered.

Sylvie crawled toward the closest car in the Rocking Wrangler parking lot. He quickly followed, keeping his body in front of hers and covering Kilo's too.

These attacks were really starting to make him mad. And now, more than ever, he believed Sean McLane was the person responsible.

CHAPTER SEVEN

When would it stop? The question flashed through her mind as she huddled behind one of the parked cars. She peered around the edge of the vehicle, hoping no one had been hurt.

"Stay down, I've called 911." Dawson crowded against her, using his body as a shield. Something no man had ever done for her. Then again, she'd never been in danger like this before either. "Deputies should be here any minute."

On cue, sirens filled the air. She hated feeling helpless, but obviously they needed the police to secure the area.

"We must have been followed," she whispered.

"Maybe." She noticed Dawson's gaze constantly moving, ensuring that no one was getting too close. Easy to see he was now in SEAL mode, the gun an extension of his hand. "I'm thinking more along the lines that our attempt to find Sean, asking about him here at the Rocking Wrangler, was the impetus for this attack."

Sean. Her own flesh and blood, plotting against her. She'd wished the attacker was Paul Griffin, it would have been easier. She already despised him and wouldn't lose a minute of sleep if he were to be arrested.

But Sean? Her chest tightened as she tried to imagine telling her father his son had tried to hurt her. She honestly wasn't sure she could do it.

Anger followed quickly by despair washed over her. Maybe she should just give in, sell the place, and move on. To do what? She had no idea. Ranching was in her heart, in her blood.

It was all she knew.

Two squads squealed to a stop. Deputies emerged from their respective vehicles, guns drawn. She recognized Rick.

"Deputy Holmes? Dawson Steele here with Sylvie McLane. I called in the report of gunfire."

The deputies took a long moment to sweep the area before Holmes headed over. "Now what happened?"

Dawson holstered his weapon, straightened, and offered her a hand. She took it, leaning on his strength to stand. It was cute to see he how he held Kilo in one arm, the dog resting his head over Dawson's shoulder like a baby. "We were inside the Rocking Wrangler, looking for Sean McLane or his rodeo buddies, but they weren't there. As we were ready to move on, someone fired at us from the west."

"The west?" Holmes turned and peered in that direction. "How do you know?"

"I heard a thud as the bullet hit the wall of the bar." Dawson lowered Kilo to the ground of the parking lot and took the two steps to get to the structure. He ran his hands over the side of the building, then stopped. "Here's the slug."

Seeing the indentation in the wall was sobering. She glanced toward the west, there were several buildings, any of which could have been used by the shooter.

"I believe the sniper's nest is on top of the clothing store over there." Dawson gestured with his hand. "You should send someone up there to check it out. Could be that the shooter left his brass behind."

Holmes lifted a brow, then reluctantly nodded. "I guess being a SEAL you know all about that stuff."

Dawson shrugged but didn't say anything more.

"Gary, go up to the rooftop of the Western Clothing store. See if you can find any evidence of a gunman being up there." Rick turned back toward her. "You were looking for your brother?"

"Yes. I haven't seen him in a while." She did her best to sound nonchalant. "Wanted to check in to make sure he's doing okay."

"Or to see if he's the one behind these incidents?" Rick asked dryly. "I had the same idea. I stopped by the Timber Inn earlier, but he wasn't there."

The news surprised her. "Oh, I thought Sean was staying with one of his rodeo buddies, Matt or Ned."

"Matt Keagan or Ned Burns," Dawson helpfully clarified. "Do you know them?"

"Sure, I know them. Unfortunately, no one has seen them around in the past few days either. The clerk said they had been staying at the inn but took off a couple of days ago." Holmes sighed and tipped the brim of his hat back. "Gotta say, I don't like what's going on here, Sylvie. Not one bit."

Join the club, she thought grimly.

Holmes took a moment to dig the bullet out of the wall, then dropped it into a small evidence bag. "Stay here, I need to interview other witnesses."

Dawson nodded in agreement, but she frowned. "We can't stay long. We need to get back to the ranch."

"Soon," Dawson promised. "I want to see if they find anything up on the roof."

She looked at the building, grimacing as she saw the deputy walking around up there. "You really think that's where the bullet came from?"

"Yes." He sounded confident.

"Did you see something?" It would explain Dawson's quick reflexes when the gunfire rang out.

"Not really, maybe a brief flash from my peripheral vision." He rubbed his abdomen, and she knew all this running and ducking for cover was taking a toll on him. "I think Gary has found something."

The deputy was on his knees, then slowly rose to his feet. From where they were standing, they could see he reached for the radio on his collar.

Holmes was just a few feet away, he'd been talking to an older couple, but turned away when his radio squawked. "Boss? Found a shell casing."

"Anything else?" Holmes asked.

"Nope. Just the casing."

"Talk to the store owners and managers, someone must have seen him go up onto the roof."

"Negative, boss. There's an old fire escape staircase on the side of the building. Perp could have gotten up and back down without anyone inside the shop seeing him."

Rick muttered something harsh under his breath. "Interview them anyway." Then he turned and came back toward them, eyeing Dawson. "You were right about the location of the shooter. Do you have additional insight you'd like to share?"

It took a moment for her to realize Deputy Holmes was asking for Dawson's help in the investigation. Oddly enough, it made her feel better to know Holmes was willing to accept whatever expertise the former Navy SEAL had to offer.

Dawson scanned the area, then slowly shook his head. "I don't, no. But this guy must have been here in town. I'm sure no one followed us here from the ranch."

That made her frown. "How can you be so sure?"

Dawson turned toward her. "I kept a keen eye on the rearview mirror. One good thing, the terrain is relatively flat coming into town. Trust me, if someone had been tailing us, I'd have noticed."

She believed him.

"Okay, so your suspect was here in town, saw you, and what, managed to get up on the roof in enough time to fire the shot?" A hint of doubt crept into Holmes's tone. "Seems like a coincidence."

"Not if you take into consideration the time we spent inside the Rocking Wrangler," Dawson drawled. "Someone could have seen us go inside, then went up to the roof to wait for us to come out."

His theory spoken in such a matter-of-fact tone made her shiver. She didn't want to imagine Sean hunting her like some animal.

Yet that's exactly what had taken place here. Because Dawson was right. If they hadn't been followed, Sean or one of his buddies must have seen them go inside the bar. Plenty of time, then, for one of them to get set up on the rooftop.

Had the bullet been intended for her? Or had the gunman purposely missed? Either way, the shooter was lucky he hadn't hit an innocent bystander.

"Do you need anything else?" Dawson asked. "I'd like to get Sylvie home."

"I thought we were going to check the Timber Inn?"

"No sense in doing that, even if Sean or his buddies

were there, they're long gone now." Dawson again spoke with confidence. "Besides, Holmes checked earlier, remember?"

She let out a heavy sigh. "Okay, fine. It's better for us to head back to the ranch anyway."

"I'd like a police escort." Dawson pinned Holmes with a steely look. "Too much wide-open space for someone to take another shot at us along the way."

The chief deputy hesitated, then nodded. "Sure thing." He turned away and asked for additional help to respond to the scene. "When Gary gets back, we'll hit the road."

"Easy, boy," Dawson murmured to Kilo. No surprise the dog stayed close to his owner's side.

"He didn't bark or growl." She knelt on the ground beside Kilo, stroking his fur. "Makes me wish I had a dog."

"What happened to Sparky?"

Surprised he'd remembered the black and white border collie they'd had when she was growing up, she offered a lopsided smile. "We had to put him down eight years ago, cancer."

"Eight years is a long time, why didn't you get another dog?"

She shook her head. "I don't know. We talked about it but never found the time to find one." She gave Kilo one last pat and stood. "You really think Sean or his buddies are staked out somewhere along the highway waiting for us?"

"SEALs are always prepared for the worst-case scenario." He draped a casual arm around her shoulders. "Let's go."

Holmes finished updating Gary, then walked them over to the SUV. Dawson put Kilo in the back, taking a moment to open a bottle of water to fill a small bowl. Kilo downed the water in ten seconds flat.

Neither of them said much as they took the highway back to McLane Mountain, following Holmes who led the way.

She felt exhausted, more so than usual. The attacks kept her on edge, and she couldn't deny the lingering fear that another one was right around the corner.

When they finally reached the ranch, she pushed out of the passenger side door, then opened the back to grab the fuel gauge. Dawson let Kilo out, then spoke to the deputy for a few minutes, before catching up to her.

"Where are you going?"

"To fix the chopper." She glanced at him. "I'm thinking we may need to do a flyover of the property, see if we can spot a possible campsite. Whoever is doing these things may be living on the mountain."

"Do you need help? I learned a bit about choppers when I got my pilot's license."

"No. I'd rather be alone." She couldn't explain the need to get away. To leave everything behind. Since leaving the ranch wasn't an option, she'd seek temporary refuge in the hangar. She turned and walked away.

Once the bird was repaired, she'd need to find her brother. Soon. Before the sheriff's deputies did.

Before the harm he'd inflicted became insurmountable.

DAWSON HATED SEEING Sylvie looking so forlorn. Her insistence on being left alone stung, but he shook it off. Obviously, she was struggling with the knowledge that her brother had taken another shot at her.

He silently agreed that Sean was at the top of the

suspect list, but one thing he'd learned as a SEAL was to never take things at face value.

The shooter hadn't hit them earlier today, the same way he hadn't hit Sylvie the day before on the north ridge. Maybe he'd missed on purpose, or maybe he was just a bad shot. The latter wasn't likely, everyone in Montana, girls and boys alike, were taught how to fire a rifle at an early age. Mostly out of necessity as bear, wolf, and cougar attacks were not uncommon.

Most Montana residents would hit what they aimed at.

It made him curious about her ex-husband, Paul Griffin. Had the guy grown up in the area? She'd mentioned he worked the ranch for a year before they got married, but that didn't mean he was an expert marksman.

He headed back to check on the progress Josh and the ranch hands had made on the barn. He was glad to see they were working hard, putting up the studs to frame the roof. At this rate, they'd have it done before nightfall.

The idea of checking into Paul Griffin wouldn't leave him alone. He decided to head back inside to get the laptop Sylvie had loaned him the night before. It felt strange to walk into a house that didn't belong to him. And he was surprised to find Connor in the kitchen.

"How are you feeling?" Dawson asked.

"Weak, as usual." Sylvie's father sounded cranky.

"It must be hard," he agreed. "I—uh, need to grab something from the guest room."

Connor nodded. "Go ahead. Where's Sylvie?"

"Replacing the fuel gauge on the chopper." He wondered if that wasn't a job that Connor could have handled himself but tried to give the older man the benefit of the doubt. It couldn't be easy to recover from prostate cancer. "Did you need something?"

"Nah, just curious." Connor poured himself a glass of iced tea. "Looks like the barn is coming along."

"Yes, sir." He didn't want to be rude, but he also wanted to look up Paul Griffin again on social media. Maybe he could swing through Sylvie's office to search for a picture of the guy.

"Josh claims he doesn't know who started the fire," Connor continued. "I told him he needed to make sure the ranch hands understood there's no smoking near the barn."

He nodded, deciding to honor Sylvie's wishes by not mentioning the more likely scenario of the fire being started on purpose.

Connor sipped his tea, then pinned him with a direct gaze. "You home to stay?"

The question caught him off guard. "I don't know the answer to that. I've been in the military for a long time, and we never stayed in one place."

"Landon wants you to take over the Copper Creek."

"I know, we've discussed it." Dawson was a little perturbed that Connor was poking his nose into his business. Then he realized this line of questioning was more about Sylvie. "Your daughter is an amazing woman, but we're just friends."

Connor grimaced. "She needs help running the place. I had hoped Paul would do that, but . . ." He shrugged.

"How well did you know Paul?"

"About as well as I know any of the ranch hands. He was a hard worker and respectful. But that didn't last."

"Do you have any pictures of him?"

Connor hiked a brow. "Interested in the competition?"

"I told you Sylvie and I are just friends." Although there was a kernel of truth to the accusation. He was curious about the guy who'd married Sylvie. And who had been so stupid to have lost her.

"I have a wedding photo of them." Connor pushed to his feet. "Come on, I'll show you."

He squelched a flash of guilt as he followed Sylvie's father to his room. The older man dug around in a drawer, then pulled out the framed photo. Dawson took it and immediately recognized Paul Griffin as one of the three men he'd found on social media last night. Then he looked at the guy more closely. He was probably considered handsome by most women, but Dawson wasn't impressed. Granted, he might feel differently if he hadn't heard how the guy had tried to take advantage of Sylvie.

"I wasn't surprised when Sylvie kicked him out," Connor admitted. "I'd been hoping for grandkids, yet it was clear Paul wasn't interested in running the ranch as much as he wanted to live off the income. The affair he had with one of the female ranch hands, though, was the kicker."

"Affair?" Dawson frowned. Sylvie hadn't mentioned anything about an affair.

"Yeah, Josh caught him in the act." Connor sighed. "I'm glad she tossed him out. My girl deserves the best."

"Yes, she does." Dawson handed the picture back. "Thanks for sharing, but I need to get back to work."

"Sure thing." Connor waved him off. "Don't mind me."

He hesitated, torn between keeping the older man company and finding Paul Griffin. He turned and went to the guest room. After tucking the laptop under his arm, he used his phone to call his father. "Connor McLane could use a visit when you have time."

"Tell him I'll stop by tomorrow," his dad said. "We're busy today moving cattle."

Another flash of guilt hit hard. Here he was about to

research Sylvie's ex when he should be helping his own father. "Do you need my assistance?"

"Been handling the ranch alone for over twenty years, haven't I?" There was an edge to his father's tone.

"You have, yes. I know Max has been shouldering a lot of the work. Look, I need to go, I'll check in with you later, okay?"

"Okay. Huh? Yeah, Max, I'm ready . . . ," his father said before disconnecting from the line.

He stared at his phone for a minute, realizing Max deserved the Copper Creek far more than he did. And it wasn't as if he needed the money. Not that being a SEAL paid a lot, but he hadn't had much time to spend what he'd earned either. And since he'd retired, the checks kept being deposited every month.

He set up the computer on the kitchen table and quickly found Sylvie's ex. Several posts indicated he was glad to be in Boulder. It made Dawson feel as if that's where the guy was originally from.

And none of the posts proved he was actually in Boulder. The mountains off in the distance were too far away to see clearly. The Rocky Mountains stretched through many states. Including Montana.

The battery was running low, so he shut it down and returned the device to the docking station in Sylvie's office. A quick glance confirmed there were no photographs of her and Paul. Understandable, especially after hearing about the affair.

He walked back outside and saw Sylvie coming toward him. She had a streak of grease along her cheek, but her smile indicated she'd successfully replaced the fuel pump.

"The chopper is up and running."

"Good for you." He used his thumb to wipe away the

grease. "I don't think I've ever met a more competent woman, and since there were several highly regarded female officers in the navy, that's saying something."

She blushed and rubbed her hands over her cheeks, removing the rest of the grease. "Thanks, but you know this is all part of a rancher's life."

Not all ranches had their own chopper, the Copper Creek certainly didn't, but he nodded anyway. If not for his stint as a SEAL, he wouldn't know how to fly a bird. Normally, SEALs weren't cross-trained to fly choppers, but he'd been curious and had gotten a few private lessons from a navy pilot friend. The guy had insisted Dawson also learn how to do minor repairs, citing that as a necessity to being a pilot.

"When do you want to head up?" He glanced up, noting the sky was clear. "I assume you want to fly over the ranch today yet."

"I do." She glanced at her watch. "Maybe after dinner."

There would be plenty of daylight left, so he nodded. "Do you mind if I ask how you know Paul Griffin is in Boulder? Is that where he grew up?"

"Yes, his family is there." She frowned. "Why?"

He decided to fill her in on his thoughts. "The shooter missed you twice now, and that's unusual for someone who grew up here, like your brother. Made me wonder if Paul is the one behind these attacks."

She pursed her lips for a moment. "It's a good point, I can't say that I ever saw Paul shoot a gun. I assumed he could, as the ranch hands always carry a rifle when they head up into the mountains, but it's possible Paul isn't good at hitting his mark." A rare smile creased her features. "Or maybe I should say, making his jack."

He grinned. "Yep, that's the proper way of saying it."

"Says you," she teased. Whatever time she'd spent alone seemed to have given her an emotional boost. "Come on, I want to check the progress inside the barn."

They headed over, Kilo romping at his side. Josh and another ranch hand were standing and looking up at the now finished roof.

"Looks great," Sylvie said. "You guys did good today."

"Thanks." Josh waved a hand toward the corral. "I assume you want the horses inside for the night."

"I do." Sylvie frowned. "Hopefully, they'll settle in all right. There's a lingering scent of smoke."

"We're on it." Josh turned and headed for the corral with the ranch hand close on his heels.

"It occurs to me that the horses might have reacted to a stranger attempting to move them out of the barn." He glanced at Sylvie. "I don't think any of your horses would recognize Max Wolfe, do you?"

"They might. Every time your dad comes to visit, we put his horse in the barn with the others." She shrugged. "The same way we put Diamond in there too. Storm might be the only one who would react to a stranger, but if the mares and other horses were taken out first, he'd probably go along. And keep in mind, we sometimes share ranch hands."

They watched the guys bring in the horses. He sensed Sylvie wanted to do her share, but she looked so exhausted he doubted she'd be much help.

"Come on, I'm hungry." He gently eased her toward the ranch house.

The beef stew had been cooking on low all day, the meat proving to be nice and tender. He filled two bowls and carried them to the table.

Sylvie picked up her fork, then set it back down. "Sorry, I know you like to say grace."

"I do." He took her hand. "Dear Lord, we are thankful for this food and for the way You have kept us safe. Please continue to watch over us as we seek the person responsible. Amen."

"Amen." Sylvie's voice was a husky whisper. She squeezed his hand before letting it go.

They ate in silence for a few minutes. He didn't want to ruin the camaraderie between them, but he had to ask, "Are you sure this is Sean's doing and not Paul's?"

She frowned. "I'm not sure of anything. But Paul would be lashing out in revenge, and to be honest, I can't imagine him being good enough to slip in and out of the ranch without someone spotting him."

"He worked here for a year, though, so it's not like he isn't familiar with the place." He hesitated, then added, "I heard about his affair. I'm sorry you had to go through that."

"Affair?" Her head shot up, her gaze drilling into him. "What are you talking about?"

"Ah," he tried to backpedal. "Your father mentioned Paul was caught in the act by Josh . . ."

"What?" She shot out of her seat. "I never heard anything about an affair." She left her half-eaten meal and stalked outside, no doubt to confront Josh.

Dawson groaned and quickly followed. "Come, Kilo. I have a feeling this isn't going to be pretty."

Yet as he hurried after Sylvie, he tried to understand why on earth Josh or her father would keep something as blatant as an affair a secret?

CHAPTER EIGHT

Why was she the last one to know Paul had an affair? So typical of the men on this ranch to keep stuff from her. Well, enough was enough. Granted, Paul's actions didn't much matter anymore, but that wasn't really the point.

Sylvie found Josh caring for the horses in the barn. "What is this I hear about Paul having an affair?"

The flash of guilt in Josh's eyes told her all she needed to know. It was true. Yet no one had bothered to tell her. She should have gotten tested at the very least. "I—uh, found him with April. You remember her, right?"

"Yeah." April had been one of their few female ranch hands. Hiring April and Jen had been her idea. She'd thought it would be good for the guys to have women working alongside them, proving they were just as capable as they were.

But she hadn't anticipated Paul would have done something so blatant as to sleep with one of them. Maybe both.

"Look, Sylvie, I told your father, and he was going to talk to you. And I thought he did because it was only a week or two later that you kicked Paul out."

His explanation only made it worse. "Why wouldn't you come to me, Josh? He was my husband, and I was the one who needed to know. Not my father!" Her voice rose to the point she was shouting at him now.

"Easy, Sylvie," Dawson's voice said from behind her.

She spun around and glared at him. "Not your business, Steele." Then she turned back to face Josh. "Did it ever occur to you that I should get tested to make sure he didn't pass along some kind of disease?"

A flush crept over Josh's features, as if discussing such things was uncomfortable for him. Seriously? They worked a ranch, mating was part of their everyday life. She stepped closer and punched her finger into his chest. "How long was it going on?"

Josh took a step back as if desperate to get away from her. "I don't know, probably not long. She left a few days later, and I figured that was because he gave her the boot."

She had to fight the urge to stab him in the chest again. "Get out. I'll finish with the horses."

"I—um—ah, pretty much finished up." Josh was almost babbling now. "I'm sorry, Sylvie. I really thought your father told you."

"I should have heard it from you!" She forced the words through clenched teeth.

"Go on, Josh, I'll help her finish up here," Dawson said.

"I don't need your help." She thrust her fingers through her hair, realizing she was acting like a bratty kid, but what part of her wanting to be alone didn't they understand? "Just go. Both of you. Leave me alone."

Josh eased around her like she was a rattlesnake ready to strike. Once Josh and Dawson left, she went over to stroke Fanny. "Men are idiots," she said to the mare. Fanny raised and lowered her head, letting out a whinny in agreement.

After a few minutes, she went from stall to stall, checking the horses. Josh had taken care of them, so there wasn't anything more for her to do. Still, she lingered.

Humiliating that Josh and her father knew about Paul's affair while she didn't. And really, why would her father mention it to Dawson? She lifted her gaze to the top of the barn as if seeking answers.

None were forthcoming.

Fifteen minutes later, she closed the barn and headed back up to the ranch house. Her flash of anger had faded, leaving her more exhausted than ever. She knew better than to pilot the chopper when she wasn't at her best. Flying over the ranch to search for her brother and his buddies would have to wait until tomorrow.

Thankfully, there was no sign of Dawson as she entered the kitchen. His SUV was still outside, so she knew he hadn't left. She could hear the TV from her dad's room, but she wasn't in the mood to talk to him either. It made her cheeks burn that he knew about Paul's blatant disregard for their wedding vows yet hadn't mentioned it.

Shaking her head, she decided she needed to get some sleep. Despite the lingering daylight outside thanks to the summer solstice, she went to her room. A hot shower eased her aches and soothed her temper. After drying her hair, she went to bed.

She slept like a rock, waking up feeling refreshed as the early morning sunlight filtered through her window. The dawn of a new day gave her hope they'd get to the bottom of whoever was behind these relentless attacks.

If Sean was the one responsible, she'd find him at one of

his favorite camping spots. It shouldn't take long to pin him down. She quickly dressed and headed to the kitchen.

Dawson was at the stove cooking breakfast. The way he pitched in to help was sweet, and she felt bad about how she'd lashed out at him in anger the night before. "Something smells great."

"Good morning." He smiled and gestured to the coffee pot. "Help yourself. Food will be ready shortly."

"You know cooking for me isn't your job." She poured a large mug of coffee. "But thank you."

"Hey, I like to eat too." He tossed a bit of bacon to Kilo who caught it midair. The dog inhaled the morsel, then licked his chops as if anticipating more.

"We'll do the early morning chores first, then take up the chopper."

"Works for me." Dawson had two fry pans going. Since it seemed he had it under control, she leaned against the counter and watched him. There was something sexy about a man who cooked for his woman.

Whoa, where had that thought come from? She wasn't Dawson's woman. Sure, he kissed like no one's business, but that didn't mean she had any intention of becoming involved with him. She knew he wasn't sticking around Dillon, Montana.

And she wasn't leaving. At least, not voluntarily. In a pine box? Maybe.

Sylvie told herself to enjoy the camaraderie while it lasted. One thing was for sure, Dawson wasn't going anywhere until they'd caught the assailant.

Likely, her brother.

"Ready?" Dawson asked. She realized he was holding two plates brimming with food.

"Oh yeah." She crossed to the table, taking the seat next

to him. She knew his prayer routine by now and waited for him to start.

"May I take your hand?" His formal request made her blush.

"You never asked before," she reminded him, placing her hand in his.

"You were pretty steamed last night, I didn't want to risk getting slapped."

"I didn't slap anyone." She narrowed her gaze in warning. "But keep it up and you will risk getting punched."

Dawson's grin only widened, then he gently squeezed her hand and bowed his head. "Dear Lord, we thank You for this wonderful food we are about to eat. We also thank You for keeping us safe in Your care and ask for Your continued guidance as we seek those who wish us harm. Amen."

"Amen." She tugged her hand from his. "I have a good feeling about today. I'm sure we'll find Sean's camping spot."

"You're sure your brother is involved?" Dawson munched a slice of bacon. Kilo stretched out on the floor between them, but when Dawson frowned at the dog, he laid his head between his paws.

She shrugged. "I'm not sure about anything, but it seems the more likely scenario."

"I have to agree, although I'm keeping your idiot ex on my list too."

They ate in silence for a few minutes. The food was delicious. She felt better prepared to face the day by the time they'd finished.

"Give me a few minutes to do the dishes," Dawson said as he carried his plate to the sink.

"I'll do it," she protested. "You take care of Kilo."

He hesitated, then nodded. "Okay. Come, Kilo."

They yellow lab jumped up, tail wagging as he followed Dawson outside. The kitchen seemed unusually empty after they left, but she told herself to get over it. She was just finishing when her dad came in with his empty plate.

"Where's Dawson?"

"Outside with Kilo." She should have realized Dawson had made breakfast for her dad too. She took the plate from his hands and quickly washed it. "We'll probably take the chopper up later this morning."

Her father nodded. "Okay."

She glanced at him, a bit concerned that he hadn't asked more questions. It was as if he'd given up all interest in running the ranch.

It made her wonder if her father secretly wanted to sell the ranch too. The way Sean did. Was she the odd man out? Was she holding on to something the other two didn't want?

She shook off the depressing thoughts. "Have you spoken to Landon Steele?"

"Not yet. I'll call him later, after the early morning chores are finished." Her father filled a coffee cup, then sat at the table. He eyed her over the rim of his mug. "Nice of Dawson to make breakfast."

"Yes, it was." She inwardly groaned, knowing her father was already thinking she and Dawson were some sort of an item. "He's a great guy, but I'm not sure he's here in Montana to stay."

"Hrmph." Her father scowled. "He needs to take his place as rightful owner of the Copper Creek."

Dawson's plans weren't her concern. Or rather, they shouldn't be her concern. She finished washing and drying the dishes. She was itching to get outside but took a moment to sit beside her father. "Have you spoken to Sean lately?"

"No." Her father shrugged. "I'm not worried. I'm sure he'll come back soon enough."

Yeah, when I am hurt or lying in a hospital bed, she thought sourly. She drained her cup and stood. "I need to get to work. Call Landon, I'm sure he'll make time to stop by for a visit."

"Yeah, yeah." Her father waved her away. As she headed outside, she realized her father hadn't left the house in several days. Granted, the chemo and radiation treatments had taken a toll on his strength, but sitting inside all day wasn't good for him either.

She suppressed a sigh. As if she didn't have enough to worry about, now this. She made a mental note to drag her father outside, gently forcing him to take over some of the less taxing chores once they returned from searching for her wayward brother.

Dawson met up with her, Kilo trotting happily at his side. She noticed he'd taken to wearing his gun holstered on his lean hip and found that oddly comforting. "Let's get to work. The sooner we get the chopper up, the better."

She nodded, and they walked to the barn. Josh was up on one of the geldings, Tucker. He flushed when he saw her but didn't mention anything about the previous night. "Sylvie, we're heading out to move the cattle from the south pasture to the east."

"Good. We'll take care of things here." She glanced at Dawson. "After we clean the horses' stalls, we'll gather eggs from the chicken coop."

"Sounds like fun," he drawled.

It wasn't, but his comment made her laugh. And working alongside Dawson made the time go by much faster. Looking back, she should have realized her marriage to Paul wasn't meant to be. He'd never worked alongside her like this.

Enough. She wasn't going to waste another second thinking about Paul. Easier to do if she didn't have Dawson standing next to her, whistling cheerfully as he mucked out Fanny's stall.

Dawson, who seemed to be everything Paul wasn't, and more.

SYLVIE SEEMED to be in a better mood this morning, and he was glad she wasn't the type to hold on to her anger. Ranch chores didn't seem so bad when they were shared, and roughly ninety minutes later, they were finished.

"I'll leave Kilo with your dad," he said, after they'd washed up. "I'm sure your dad won't mind."

"He won't. In fact, you need to tell him to take Kilo outside often, like every hour or so. Dad needs to get out more, he's been sitting around inside for too long."

"Done." He looked down at Kilo. "Come on, boy."

Ten minutes later, they were headed for the chopper. Sylvie stopped just outside the hangar and turned to look up at him. "I'd like you to pilot the bird, Dawson, so I can search the mountainside."

"Sounds good to me." He was more than happy to take the stick. "I hope we find something."

"Me too." Her tone sounded grim.

He pulled the chopper out of the hangar and onto the landing pad. He went around the bird, doing a quick maintenance check, finding the machine in good shape. He had to give Sylvie credit for the way she handled every aspect of the ranch.

And hated to admit how much it bugged him that she had to do so much alone. Sure, Josh was there, along with a half dozen ranch hands, but a place this size needed more.

Once they were seated, headphones covering their ears, he went through the preflight check. Sylvie did, too, as a double check. When he was satisfied, he started the engine. The blades whirled overhead, and it didn't take much to get airborne.

"Where would you like to start?" he asked via the intercom.

"North ridge," Sylvie said, gesturing to the right. "But don't get too close to the mountain."

"Roger that." He understood the danger. After banking the chopper around a curve, he headed toward the north ridge. From up here, the lizard trail looked even more treacherous. Way down at the bottom of the trail, he could see the boulder that had nearly hit them.

He kept the bird as low as possible while staying clear of the tree line. Thankfully, there very little wind to worry about.

Sylvie peered out her window, intently scanning the side of the mountain.

"Why the north ridge?" He glanced over her shoulder to see what may have caught her attention.

She didn't answer right away. "There's a shallow cave, not far from the lizard trail. We used to camp there during the summer. Figure that may be where Sean is hiding out."

Maybe, but if Sean was smart, he'd know Sylvie would think to search for him there. Dawson didn't point that out, though. Better to focus on the task of flying.

He made two passes over the north ridge without success. "Head to the west side now," Sylvie directed.

He did as she asked, moving along the western part of

the mountain. The terrain was rougher there; he could see evidence of some small landslides raking down the steepest side of the mountain. Maybe the boulder hadn't been pushed.

They flew for another ten minutes before Sylvie sat back in her seat. "I don't see him, but that doesn't mean he isn't down there."

"I know." He felt bad, yet he also knew that if Sean had heard the chopper, he'd lie low until they were gone. "Maybe we should put the bird down somewhere and go on foot."

"Not yet." She turned to meet his gaze. "Sweep over the pastures, I want to check on the cattle Josh is moving."

"You're the boss." He banked the chopper in a curve to fly over the wide-open pasture. McLane Mountain hugged the ranch on the north and western sides, but the rest of the property consisted of wide, green pastures extending for miles.

It was easy to spot Josh and the ranch hands as they drove the cattle from one pasture to the next. The herd was triple the size his father had.

Sylvie nodded in approval. "Looking good."

"You want me to swing past the north ridge one more time?" He wasn't sure how much fuel she wanted to waste in searching for her brother.

"Yeah." She turned and peered out her window again.

He expected to do just one more sweep, but then she grabbed his arm. "Wait! I see something."

"What?"

"A flash of red not far from the lizard trail, but in the opposite direction of the cave." She didn't turn to look at him. "Can you get a little closer?"

"Yep." He banked the chopper to take another pass.

Then he saw it too. Just a glimpse, but definitely something red. A man wearing a red shirt and blue jeans perhaps. It was hard to tell for sure because the color disappeared from sight.

Wouldn't Sean know better than to wear red in the middle of the woods in June? Or had Sylvie's younger brother just assumed she wouldn't suspect him as the person responsible for the attacks?

"We need to put the bird down," Sylvie said. "I want to search the area on foot."

"We won't be able to get too close," he warned.

"I know. Just put it down at the edge of the pasture."

He nodded and looked for the flattest section of the terrain, without getting too close to the edge of the mountain. He slowly lowered the helicopter to the location he'd chosen, setting it down with a mild thump.

"Nice work." Sylvie ripped the headphones off as he shut down the engine. She shoved open her door. "Grab a water bottle from the back."

He peered over his shoulder and took two bottles, handing one to her.

"Thanks. Let's go."

"It's farther than it looks," he cautioned as they set out.

"I know that." She arched a brow. "It's not likely we'll find the person wearing a red shirt, but I feel confident we'll find his campsite."

"Okay." He followed Sylvie up the side of the mountain, wishing he'd brought Kilo along after all. The yellow lab had a good nose for scent tracking. Granted, he'd only done a little scent training with Kilo because the series of abdominal surgeries had interrupted his routine, making it difficult to maintain consistency. It wasn't long after his last procedure that his dad had requested help at the ranch.

The terrain was rocky, the hillside steep. Yet Sylvie hiked it without seeming to break a sweat. He kept up, reassured by the way she seemed to know where she was going.

Easy to imagine she and Sean had spent a fair amount of time on the mountain. They walked for roughly twenty minutes before she paused to rest.

"Any sign of a campsite?" He tried not to let his heavy breathing show as he took a sip from the water bottle. Painful to admit that he'd been in the best shape of his life while serving the navy, only to have a gut load of shrapnel age him by well over ten years. He was glad he was armed in case they stumbled across any wildlife. Or two-legged varmints.

"Not yet." She grimaced and took a swig from her water bottle. "But we will. At the very least, we'll find evidence of a guy hiking out here."

"Maybe I should lead the way." He replaced the cap on his bottle and gazed at her. "I've had some practice in tracking hostiles."

She looked as if she might argue, then surprised him by nodding. "Okay, that's fine. I'm sure as a former Navy SEAL you're a far better tracker than I am."

"Okay, which direction? Do you still want to head up the side of the mountain or spread out a bit?"

She considered his question. "I say we keep going up the mountain for now."

"Sounds good. Ready?" He didn't want to be the one holding them back.

"Lead on." She stepped back so he could pass by.

He took a moment to get his bearings, then headed up the barely visible trail. He searched for signs of a human being there recently but didn't see anything unusual. Maybe he shouldn't have boasted about his tracking ability.

God didn't like a braggart. He lifted his heart and silently prayed for the wisdom to find the attacker before he struck again.

They walked for roughly ten minutes before he saw it. A very tiny tuft of red clinging to a pricker bush. He stopped and bent to examine it more closely. There wasn't a doubt in his mind that it was a snag from a red shirt.

"He came this way," Sylvie said in satisfaction. "Good eye, Dawson."

He could feel his cheeks redden at her praise, which was ridiculous. "Thanks, but we still haven't found his campsite."

"We will." Her voice rang with confidence. "Let's keep going. We must be headed in the right direction."

He thought so too, so he nodded and continued hiking. His abdominal muscles ached as they continued up the mountain, but he did his best to ignore it. Stopping wasn't an option, and it seemed as if pain would be his constant companion for a while.

He stopped again when he found a partial hiking boot print in the soft soil. "Check this out, Sylvie."

"Yeah, it's a hiking boot, not unlike the ones we're wearing." She knelt beside it for a moment, then looked up at him. "What do you think? Are we close to the spot where we saw him from the chopper?"

He turned to look back the way they'd come. The bird was sitting roughly two hundred yards below them. They'd come farther than he'd thought. Lifting his gaze to the sky, he checked out the west mountain ridge. "Not quite. I believe we saw him higher up than this. But we're on the right track."

"Let's keep going." She sounded energetic, which only made him feel older than his thirty-nine years.

He turned and headed up. They hit a particularly steep spot, and he had to grab onto small tree branches to keep from sliding backward into Sylvie. He was about to call off the climb when the terrain leveled out.

"I remember this place," Sylvie said. For the first time on this hike she sounded breathless. "If we go to the west, there's an area that's even wider, and there's a rock there that provides some shelter from the wind."

"You think that might be where the campsite is located?"

Her green gaze held his. "There's only one way to find out."

He pulled his weapon from its holster and was glad he'd also brought the MK 3 knife favored by the SEALs.

If they were walking into a trap, he wanted to be ready.

"I'll go first." Sylvie's voice had dropped to a whisper. Since she knew the area and the place they were headed, he nodded in agreement.

They moved slower now, taking care not to make noise. He listened intently as they approached but didn't hear anything unusual.

Sylvie's steps slowed, then she paused near a tree. He went up to stand behind her. The large rock she'd mentioned was only twenty feet away.

And below the rock was a sleeping bag and a small firepit. There wasn't a doubt in his mind that this was the campsite of the man in the red shirt. Unfortunately, there was no sign of the guy.

Dawson hoped and prayed the guy wasn't lying in wait to ambush them.

CHAPTER NINE

Raking her gaze over the campsite, Sylvie didn't see anything that indicated the man in the red shirt was Sean. The green sleeping bag wasn't anything unusual, it looked like the typical bed roll that every ranch hand owned. There were no glowing embers in the small firepit, but she needed to get closer to see if the debris was still warm.

She moved to stand, but Dawson grabbed her arm and tugged her down. "Wait," he whispered. "Could be a trap."

A trap? She frowned and scanned the area again. The place looked deserted, although clearly leaving his sleeping bag behind meant he was planning to return. She whispered, "We saw the guy in the red shirt moving away from the campsite."

"No, we saw him moving along the mountainside, then disappearing from view," Dawson corrected. "I'd like you to stay here while I check out the area."

It went against the grain to let Dawson go off without her, but he was a Navy SEAL. If anyone could move silently through the brush, it was him. Not to mention, he was armed. "Okay."

"Here, take this." He pressed the gun into her hand.

"You'll need it more than me," she argued.

"I have a knife, and I want you to be safe."

She scowled, but Dawson moved soundlessly into the brush before she could voice another argument. She stared at the weapon, then back at the campsite.

Okay, fine. She knew how to shoot a gun, but if the guy in the red shirt was her brother, she wouldn't need it. Sean might be feeling desperate enough to lash out at her, but she was certain she could get him to listen to reason.

She settled in to wait, impressed that she didn't see or hear Dawson making his way through the woods. She shivered a bit as she realized he must have used these same tactics while entering terrorist camps and other war zones.

He'd spent twenty years putting his life on the line for his country. As far as she knew, Dawson was the only guy from Dillon, Montana, to do so.

A squirrel jumped through the campsite, disappearing in the brush on the other side. She waited another few minutes, then eased out from behind the brush and crept toward the campsite.

Dawson's weapon was heavy in her hand. She was more accustomed to holding a rifle in a sling over her shoulder. Still, she kept it handy, prepared for anything.

She lowered her hand over the charred remains of the fire. It was warm, but not hot. Made sense, considering the time frame between when they'd seen the guy in the red shirt and had set down the bird to hike up here. Then she moved toward the sleeping bag. She tried to remember the last time she'd seen Sean's pack but couldn't. It just wasn't something she'd cared enough about to notice.

The location near the large rock, though, was a familiar

spot for her brother. They'd hiked there as kids, and it was easy to imagine Sean hiding out there.

But the campsite was still pretty far from the ranch house. Maybe too far. For Sean to get from here to the barn and back would take several hours on foot. And there was no sign of a horse being tethered nearby.

She figured it was possible he'd used a closer campsite that first night, after shooting at her when she was on the north ridge. Those moments she'd dangled off the edge of the cliff still haunted her.

Likely Sean hadn't intended for that to happen, but it also hadn't stopped him from coming after her again and again.

She shook off the lingering despair and forced herself to focus on the here and now. There was nothing else in the campsite, which was a little strange. No backpack, cooking utensils, or any other personal items. No garbage either. Frankly, that last part didn't seem like Sean at all.

With a small sigh, she crept through the campsite to return to the spot in the brush. There was a slim possibility that Sean, or whoever had camped there, would return.

Besides, Dawson had asked her to stay put.

Roughly fifteen minutes passed before she heard a twig snap. Straightening, she lifted the gun from her lap and rested it against the side of a tree. She didn't think the intruder was Dawson as she hadn't heard a sound when he'd left.

A doe stepped out of the woods. The deer sniffed the air, then abruptly turned and jumped away. No doubt the scent of charred wood from the fire had spooked her.

She lowered the weapon.

Another five minutes passed. "Sylvie?" Dawson's voice was a low whisper. "I'm coming toward you."

Surprised, she nodded and glanced around, trying to figure out which direction he was coming from. He emerged from the brush behind her.

"Find anything?"

He shook his head. "A few more signs of someone moving around, but whoever was out here is either well-hidden or managed to put a lot of distance between us."

That figured. Super frustrating to have come this far yet not find the person responsible. She gestured to the camp-site. "Just a sleeping bag, nothing else, not even an empty package of trail mix. The remnants of the fire were warm, not hot. By now they may even be cool."

Dawson's brow furrowed. "Interesting. Makes me think he was packing up to leave when he spotted the chopper. Took off without the sleeping bag to make better time."

His theory made sense. "So now what?"

"I scouted the entire area, no one is hiding nearby. But our guy could be holed up farther up the mountain." He lifted his head to the clear blue sky lightly dotted with puffy clouds. "We can hope he doesn't have a rifle scope trained on us, but if he did, I'd think he'd have taken a shot by now."

The thought wasn't at all reassuring. She glanced around apprehensively, hoping and praying if Sean was out there, he wouldn't aim to hit either of them.

"It's almost noon, so our next steps are up to you," Dawson continued. "We can keep searching or head back to the chopper."

She suppressed a sigh. Part of her wanted to keep going, but leaving the chopper unattended for this long probably wasn't good. And if the guy in the red shirt was hiding, he could be anywhere. It was amazing they'd found his camp-site. "We should head back." She handed him his weapon, butt first.

"Okay, hang on a minute, I'm grabbing that sleeping bag." He holstered his weapon, then strode into the campsite.

"Why?" she asked as he began to roll the sleeping bag into a tight ball.

"No reason to make it comfortable for this guy to sleep out beneath the stars, right?" He flashed a grin.

It was an idea that hadn't occurred to her. "Makes sense."

When Dawson had the bag rolled and secured with ties, he carried it beneath his arm. "Let's go."

She nodded, falling into step beside him. "I have a couple of PowerBars if you're hungry."

"Great, thanks."

She rummaged in her pack for the PowerBars, handing him one and keeping the other for herself. They munched on their makeshift lunch as they headed down the trail. She noticed Dawson kept looking around from side to side as they walked, stopping every so often to look up behind them.

He also took them down through the thicker brush, no doubt to keep them well-hidden from view. She had to admit, watching him in action was interesting. His training was admirable. Without seeming to think about it, he took turns and detours on the path she never would have considered.

Humbling to realize how much he cared about keeping her safe. If they did manage to find the gunman, she knew it would be due to Dawson's immense skill more than anything she'd done.

Thankfully, they made it to the bottom of the trail without incident. Still, Dawson held her back, his gaze searching the area around the chopper. When he was satisfied, he moved forward.

"I can pilot us back to the ranch," she offered.

"I'll do it, but let's make sure the bird hasn't been tampered with first." His expression was grim. "I'm wishing now that I'd have kept Kilo inside to stand guard."

"The guy we spotted was going up the mountain not down."

"He could have an accomplice."

She couldn't argue, so they both examined the bird from top to bottom. The chopper looked fine to her, but she deferred to Dawson's expertise. She imagined he'd see signs of tampering before she would.

Finally, he appeared satisfied. "Hop in. Let's get her airborne."

She climbed in, taking the copilot seat. Dawson put on his headphones, then went through the preflight routine. He fired up the engine, and seconds later, they were in the air.

"I was really hoping we'd find the guy. Sean or whoever is behind this." She continued peering through her window, hoping to catch another glimpse of the red shirt or anyone else moving around. "The campsite proves the gunman is on the ranch, but we're no closer to identifying who he is."

"I know," Dawson agreed. "I was hoping he would make a mistake, revealing himself. He must have gone much farther than I anticipated."

"Yeah." Again, it was difficult to imagine Sean being that good. Not that he wasn't a skilled camper, because he was. But savvy enough to elude a retired Navy SEAL?

No way. Sean was too impatient, too lazy, really. He wanted the easy money rather than continuing to work the ranch.

Yet she couldn't imagine Paul out there either. For the same exact reasons. If he hadn't worked for the ranch for a year, she'd wonder if he'd ever done hard labor in his life.

"What are you thinking?" Dawson asked.

She glanced at him, then went back to scouring the mountainside. "Just that Sean or Paul wouldn't be this good at evading you. Neither of them displayed that sort of patience before."

He didn't say anything for a long moment. "Money can be a powerful motivator."

"I guess." She watched the mountain for as long as she could before Dawson banked around to fly over the south pasture. It looked as if things were going well, the cattle were pretty much relocated by now.

It occurred to her that if Josh was down there moving cattle, he couldn't be the guy in the red shirt. Maybe she was wrong to suspect him. He'd fought the fire alongside her and had also stayed back at the ranch when she and Dawson had headed into Dillon.

"Satisfied?" Dawson asked.

"Yeah, thanks."

He nodded and swung the chopper toward the ranch. Ten minutes later, he gently lowered the bird onto the landing pad.

She removed her headphones and hopped out of the helicopter. Battling back a wave of frustration, she helped push the bird back into the hangar.

"You need to keep this hangar locked at all times," Dawson said as he pulled out the sleeping bag from the back.

"I always do," she agreed. "Mostly to protect the fuel. But I can see where tampering with the engine could be a problem as well." Something she hadn't ever worried about before.

"Exactly. You need to remain on high alert." Dawson pinned her with a concerned look. "Especially after finding that campsite. Someone was there, saw us, and took off. That's hardly normal behavior."

"I know." She sighed. "I'm not taking these attacks lightly, Dawson. But finding one lone camper among fifteen hundred acres of ranch is impossible."

"Hey, don't give up hope." He stepped forward and gave her a friendly hug. "We'll find him. He already made one mistake, leaving his sleeping bag behind. He'll make another one."

She nodded, but she wasn't really convinced. By the time this guy made another mistake, she might be hurt, or worse.

For a moment, she leaned against Dawson, savoring his strength. Not just the physical strength he possessed but his character. His determination to do what was right.

"Aw, Sylvie." His deep husky voice reverberated near her ear.

"I'm okay," she began, but then she couldn't talk at all because he lowered his head and captured her mouth in a deep kiss.

DAWSON KNEW KISSING Sylvie was a bad idea, but he couldn't help himself. His willpower had crumbled to dust when she'd leaned against him.

Gathering her closer still, he lost himself in her sweet taste, her warm embrace. He'd never wanted a woman the way he yearned for Sylvie. Hot desire fried his brain cells, making it impossible to think clearly.

Finally, some rational portion of his brain reminded him he was making a promise he couldn't keep. Garnering all the strength he could muster, he slowly pulled back from their kiss.

"Wow," Sylvie murmured. "I think that was better than the last one."

Male pride surged, but he tamped it down with an effort. "I—uh, don't know why I did that."

She arched a brow. "Because you wanted to, I hope."

"I do, but, Sylvie . . ." He sighed and rubbed the back of his neck. "I don't know what my future holds. And I need to stay focused on keeping you safe."

She stared at him for a long moment. "Kissing me prevents you from keeping me safe?"

"Oh, yeah. It's impossible to think clearly when you're in my arms." He purposely took a step back, although it didn't help. Her sweet taste and intoxicating scent were seared in his senses. "I can't be distracted, Sylvie, that's a sign of weakness the gunman could exploit. And I won't make a promise I can't keep."

"I don't remember asking for any promises," she responded tartly. "But thanks for clarifying things."

He inwardly groaned, hating that he'd upset her. She stalked out of the hangar, then paused, waiting with a look of impatience etched across her features. He followed her out, still carrying the sleeping bag. She closed the door, secured the lock, then headed toward the ranch house.

His stomach rumbled with hunger, the PowerBar long gone. He wondered if she'd mind him throwing together something for lunch. When she headed inside, he dropped the sleeping bag on the ground. No point in lugging it inside.

When they entered the ranch house, he found his father and Connor seated at the kitchen table eating grilled bacon, lettuce, and tomato sandwiches. Kilo rushed over to greet Dawson as if he'd been gone for days instead of hours.

"Help yourself!" Connor waved at the counter where the fixings were still spread out.

"Hi, Landon, Dad." Some of Sylvie's annoyance faded as she crossed over to give her dad a kiss on the cheek. "It's good to see you up."

"Had to take care of Kilo, didn't I?" her dad pointed out.

"Thanks for doing that." Dawson bent down to hug the lab. "I hope he didn't cause you any trouble."

"Nah, he's a good boy." Connor looked more animated and upbeat than usual. He hoped Kilo had played a role in his transformation, but he suspected his father's visit was the catalyst. Maybe Connor didn't want to be viewed as an invalid by his fellow rancher.

Whatever worked, he thought.

"Thanks for making lunch," Sylvie said, crossing to the sink. She washed up, then set about making a sandwich.

Dawson followed suit, making two thick sandwiches. As he sat beside Sylvie, he silently said grace since both his father and Sylvie's were already half finished.

"How was the flyover?" Connor asked.

"Good. Josh moved the cattle to the east pasture this morning." She glanced at Dawson as if reminding him to keep the campsite discovery a secret. He gave a slight nod, indicating he understood. "Everything else looks great."

"Glad to hear it." Connor didn't ask anything further, which surprised him a bit. Sylvie's dad was clearly not interested in the day-to-day working of the ranch.

He noticed his father frowning, too, as if coming to the same conclusion.

When they were finished eating, he noticed Connor went over to fill the sink with soapy water. Glad he was chipping in to help, Dawson led Kilo outside. He picked up the sleeping bag he'd dropped outside the ranch house and gave it to Kilo to sniff.

"Seek, Kilo. Seek!"

The lab eagerly lifted his snout and trotted around the yard. When the K9 didn't alert, Dawson carried the bag into the bunkhouse.

Everyone was out moving cattle, so Kilo had free rein. While Kilo tried to find the scent, he took a moment to check every bunk. None were missing a sleeping bag from what he could see, although he imagined there would be extras around.

There were no identifying marks on the bag, nothing to indicate it was property of the McLane Mountain Ranch. He figured Dillon's general store sold dozens just like it.

Sylvie's comments about her brother and ex-husband had caused him to rethink the culprit. Oh, not that one of them isn't behind the attacks but that they'd hired someone to do the job.

Someone who was good enough to evade him and Kilo's keen nose.

If he'd been alone on the mountainside, he'd have kept tracking the guy until he'd found him. But leaving Sylvie alone had been difficult enough, he kept expecting to hear gunfire as she defended herself.

He debated returning alone, but that would mean leaving Sylvie vulnerable, and that wasn't an option. The barn fire and the pitchfork incidents proved the ranch itself wasn't a safe haven.

Sounds of horses and men talking indicated Josh and the others were back from the east pasture. He took the sleeping bag outside and waited for the guys to approach. Josh looked at him warily as he swung out of the saddle.

"Dawson."

"Josh. I need a moment when you're finished caring for the horses."

The foreman nodded, then turned away to lead the gelding into the barn. The rest of the ranch hands followed suit.

Dawson doubted the ranch foreman would recognize the sleeping bag, but he needed to be sure. And to discuss the campsite location. It occurred to him that other ranch hands might use that area to camp too. The large outcropping of rock provided a nice shelter.

"What's going on?" Josh asked as he joined him in the bunkhouse. "I saw Sylvie up in the chopper, did she find something?"

"We both went up, and yeah, we found this." He toed the sleeping bag with his shoe. "Some guy in a red shirt was camping at a location roughly fifty yards west of the lizard trail, next to a large rock."

Josh nodded slowly. "I know the spot. Did you find him?"

"No." He waited to see if Josh would say anything more.

"Look, Dawson, I'm not sure what you're getting at, but all of my guys are accounted for."

"I thought a couple of them were off this week?"

"Yeah, okay, other than those two guys, the rest were with me today. I get why you're concerned about some squatter camping near the lizard trail, but why are you confronting me about it? I've told you from the beginning I'm not involved in whatever is going on around here."

"You recognize this bag?" Dawson asked.

Josh snorted. "Looks like a million others around here. So yeah, I guess I'd say it looks familiar."

"You know, I'd think you'd want to help keep Sylvie safe," Dawson drawled. "You'll likely be out of a job if she has to sell to some big commercial group, which is likely the only buyer that would be able to afford the hefty price tag."

"I do want Sylvie safe," Josh said defensively. "I didn't set that fire or do any of the other stuff either. I like working the Double M. It's a great ranch."

"When did you last talk to Sean?"

Josh frowned. "Two weeks ago, when he took off all fit to be tied."

"You haven't seen him hanging around?"

"No way. Besides, Sean didn't do anything more than necessary, not lazy but not highly motivated either." Josh shrugged. "I overheard him telling one of the ranch hands that as the owner he deserved better than shucking out stalls and doing other ranch work."

"All ranchers do that work."

"Yeah, like Sylvie." Josh flushed. "Look, is that all? I've got things to do."

Dawson nodded since he didn't think the guy knew anything of significance. For sure Josh wasn't the one who'd been camping near the lizard trail.

Interesting to learn Josh didn't have much respect for Sean. Most ranchers were hard workers, this life wasn't for the faint of heart. But Sean had also grown up here, so why the sudden desire to get the money and run?

He lightly smacked himself upside the head. "Come, Kilo."

The yellow lab lifted his head from where he'd been sniffing the grass and loped over to his side. As he walked to the ranch house, Sylvie came out.

"I saw you talking to Josh," she said.

"Yeah, just to ask about the campsite. But listen, you mentioned changing the bank account passwords after kicking Sean out, which begs the question, why does your brother have money troubles?"

"I—uh, never said he had trouble, but now that you mention it, he had been going through a lot of cash recently." She stared at him. "You think he has gambling debts or something?"

"Yeah. Let's go inside, I want you to show me all of Sean's cash withdrawals."

She hesitated, and he understood she wasn't keen on showing him her bank account information.

"I don't need to see your bank statements, but I would like the dates and amounts your brother took out from the account."

"It was a lot," she admitted softly. "I guess I should have thought about the fact that he was either using drugs or gambling."

"Sylvie, please. We need the details to give to Deputy Holmes. Maybe he knows about drug dealing or gambling rings going on in Dillon."

"Fine." She turned and walked back into the ranch house. He noticed his father's truck was gone, and Connor was back in his bedroom with the TV on.

Sylvie's dad needed to get out and do something constructive, sitting around all day wasn't going to cut it. He needed to have a heart-to-heart with Connor, very soon.

They went straight to Sylvie's office. He dropped into

one of the chairs, while she went behind the desk and wiggled the mouse to bring the computer to life.

She typed for a bit, then stared at the screen. Pulling a tablet of paper toward her, she began making notes.

When she finished, she sat back, her expression grim. "Ten thousand dollars."

He let out a low whistle. "Over what time period?"

"Five months." She tossed the tablet across the desk.

The dates weren't necessarily consistent. The amounts weren't either. They ranged from six hundred to over a thousand dollars, every two to three weeks.

But there wasn't a single doubt in his mind that Sean was involved in something criminal. Which made it that much more likely he or someone he hired was Sylvie's attacker.

CHAPTER TEN

A sick sense of dread curled in her stomach. How was it that she hadn't realized just how much money Sean was pulling from their account? Sure, she'd noticed, but she hadn't really taken the time to tally the amount until now.

Ten grand. What on earth would Sean want with that kind of cash?

Buying a new truck would be one lump-sum payment or regularly scheduled monthly payments. Not this hodge-podge of withdrawals.

"I'm sorry, Sylvie." Dawson reached across the desk to take her hand. "We need to get this information to Chief Deputy Holmes. This may be enough to issue an arrest warrant for your brother."

She nodded slowly, clinging to his hand for a moment. If her brother was involved in gambling or drugs, she couldn't protect him. Not after seeing the amount of money he'd gone through. No wonder the attacks against her had been escalating. Sean must be feeling desperate now that she'd cut him off.

It made her feel worse to think about what he might be

doing to make up for the loss of income. Probably nothing good, like getting a job.

"Are you okay?"

"No." She stared at their joined hands for a long moment before pulling free to use the computer keyboard. "I'll print a copy to give to Rick."

"I think you should ask Holmes to come out here." A frown puckered Dawson's brow. "I don't want a repeat of the gunfire outside the Rocking Wrangler."

Normally, she didn't like going into town, preferring to stay on the ranch. But for some reason the thought of being stuck here bothered her. Like she was the one in jail despite having done nothing wrong.

She told herself to get over it.

"Are you going to talk to your dad?"

She grimaced. "Not yet. I don't really know anything other than the missing cash. It's not like I can prove Sean is involved in something illegal. It's suspicious, yes, but there could be another explanation."

"Like what?"

The question was a good one. She had no idea.

Dawson held her gaze, then shrugged. "Up to you."

Yeah, it was her decision when to bring her father into this. And now wasn't the time. Her dad still had two more rounds of radiation to go through, the last thing he needed was additional stress.

Besides, it would be better to wait until she was able to confront her brother personally.

She pulled out her phone and made the call to Rick. He sounded very interested in the cash withdrawals and promised to be there as soon as possible.

"Josh and the rest of the ranch hands returned from the

east pasture," Dawson said. "I think we can safely cross Josh off the suspect list."

"I know, it's impossible for him to be in two places at once." She pushed away from the desk. "I'd like to go for a ride, but we should wait until Rick shows up." Rising to her feet, she took the bank paperwork from the printer, folded it, and stuffed it into her pocket. "Let's take a walk."

"Come, Kilo." Dawson and Kilo joined her.

The warm June air didn't ease the tightness in her stomach. Glancing up at the cloud-spotted sky, she thought about how Dawson prayed before every meal.

She could use some of God's strength now.

Please, Lord, help guide Sean on the right path before he goes too far astray.

"Where would you like to go?" Dawson asked.

Away, she thought. *Far, far away.* But that wasn't an option. She should be chipping in to help with the routine chores but figured they should wait until they'd talked to the deputy. "I see Storm is in his paddock. Let's visit with him."

"Fine-looking horse," Dawson drawled as they walked along the fence line. "I know he's sired some mares for us."

"Yeah, and your stallion, Rocco, has done the same here." She had to smile. "Our fathers really support each other, don't they?"

Dawson nodded. "In the early years it was a necessity to depend on your neighbors. My grandfather and yours both started these ranches, handing them down to our fathers, and ultimately to us."

She slanted him a look. "Except you don't want the Copper Creek."

He hesitated. "After being on the move for twenty

years, it's hard to imagine being tied to one place, like the ranch."

There was no reason for her to feel a stab of disappointment. Dawson hadn't kept his feelings a secret. And this was exactly what he'd meant by telling her he didn't want to make a promise he couldn't keep.

"I understand." She didn't really, but she hadn't spent twenty years in the military either. "I'm sure there's a wonderful world out there beyond Montana."

"You've never traveled outside the state?" He sounded appalled.

"I've been to Colorado and Wyoming buying horses." She shot him a wry glance. "But I'm thinking that doesn't count in your opinion."

"You'd be right," he said with a laugh. Then his expression sobered. "Unfortunately, I've seen more unpleasant places than not during my numerous deployments. It's just hard to imagine sticking in one spot for the rest of my life."

"Well, you don't have to, right? You can go wherever you'd like." She tried to sound lighthearted, as if she didn't care.

But she did. Far more than she should.

"You should visit San Diego sometime," Dawson said. "The weather is great all year round and so is being near the ocean."

She gazed up at the mountain ridge that belonged to her ranch. The ocean sounded incredible, but she couldn't imagine leaving the ranch for an extended length of time. "I bet it's amazing. Do you have a place there?"

"Not at the moment." He didn't expound on that, and she didn't ask. There was no doubt in her mind that Dawson would end up traveling from place to place, stopping at home just long enough to check on his father.

She jumped up on the edge of the fence and whistled. Storm lifted his head and trotted toward her.

"Josh rides him a fair amount, doesn't he?" Dawson asked as she stroked the stallion.

"Yeah. We're planning to keep Storm's colt, Jasper, as a future sire too." She grinned. "Last I heard, your dad was excited to mate Jasper with one of your best mares."

"I'm not surprised." Dawson patted the horse's flank, then jumped back when the stallion kicked out. "Feisty."

"I know. He isn't great with strangers, which is why Josh rides him so often. The only three people on the ranch he tolerates is me, Josh, and my dad."

"What about Sean?"

She frowned and nodded. "Sean too."

In the distance, she could see a cloud of dust. No doubt, Rick Holmes heading their way.

She sighed and reluctantly slipped down off the fence. It wasn't a good feeling to hand over information that may implicate her brother in illegal activities.

Yet she didn't have a choice. Sean needed to be held accountable for whatever mess he'd gotten himself into.

If he was only guilty of the attacks against her, she'd refuse to press charges as long as he promised not to do it again. But she didn't think that was the case.

She had a very bad feeling he was involved in something far worse.

THE LOOK of dread on Sylvie's features pained him. Dawson wished there was more he could do. The urge to pull her into his arms was so strong he found himself leaning toward her.

Yet he forced himself away. Sylvie wasn't leaving the ranch, and he wasn't staying. At least, not for long. Visits, sure, but to be in the same place day after day for months, even years on end?

Unimaginable.

Yet when he glanced at Sylvie, he could secretly admit how much he'd miss her when the danger was over. Just seeing the ranch, the stallion, everything around them through her eyes gave him a better appreciation for the wilderness around them.

She was one of the strongest women he'd ever known. And one of the most stubborn.

He wanted to find her brother, using whatever means necessary to force him into telling the truth.

They stood for a moment watching the squad approach. Kilo spotted a squirrel and took off after it, only to stop abruptly when the animal disappeared up a tree. Looking dejected, Kilo turned and trotted back to his side.

"You should consider getting your dad a dog." He glanced at Sylvie. "It would be good for your dad to have responsibilities."

"You're probably right. Maybe once this is over." She walked toward Holmes, pulling the paperwork from her back pocket. "Thanks for coming out again, Rick."

"Show me what you have," Holmes said. "Sounds serious."

"It is." Dawson quickly joined them. "Have you found Sean or his rodeo buddies yet?"

"No, it appears as if they've left town." Holmes took the paperwork from Sylvie. His brows levered up when he saw the withdrawals she'd marked for him. "Ten thousand total?"

"Yes, with change." She sighed. "I feel stupid for not

realizing how much he'd pulled out of the account sooner. I guess I was distracted by my dad's illness and running the ranch."

"We've been hearing about illegal gambling taking place in Dillon," Holmes admitted. "There's always been the usual sports pools, but rumor going around town is that there are big stakes poker games going on."

"Have you noticed outsiders milling about?" Dawson asked. "Could be that Dillon was targeted by someone looking to make a killing."

"Now that you mention it, yeah, there have been some new faces. Many of them have come and gone. Although one guy in particular claims to be looking for property to buy. Reba, the real estate agent, has shown him everything that's for sale, but he hasn't been satisfied with what she's offered." Holmes shook his head. "Call me crazy, but it seems suspicious to me. We've tried to keep an eye on the guy, but he hasn't broken any laws that we're aware of. At least not yet."

Not yet was the operative phrase, Dawson thought.

"I sure hate to think Sean got himself tangled up with Ben Stuart," Holmes added. "Can't trust an outsider."

He filed the name away for future reference, although he knew that Stuart being an outsider didn't mean anything. Plenty of people wanted to invest in property, even in the wilderness of Montana.

"Where exactly is this illegal gambling taking place?" Sylvie's question interrupted his thoughts. "The Rocking Wrangler?"

"That's one possibility, but I've heard the Timber Inn and the Beaverhead Grill also mentioned." Holmes shrugged. "It's been difficult to get anyone to talk; so far, all we're getting are denials. From what we can tell, all the games are held after hours."

"Was Sean gone overnight?" Dawson looked at Sylvie. "Bar time is two in the morning, if the poker games are starting then, they're probably not finished until dawn."

"I honestly don't know." She blew out a heavy sigh. "Sean didn't fill me in on his comings and goings. Sure, I often saw Sean in the morning, and some days he looked worse than others, as if he could have been up late drinking. But I was focused on running the ranch and taking Dad in for treatments."

"I'm sure Josh would have mentioned if Sean wasn't doing his fair share."

She let out a harsh laugh. "Yeah, Josh was none too happy about Sean. And that's the main reason I told Sean he had a choice, either work the ranch to earn his pay or be cut off." She shrugged. "You know how that went."

"You cut him off." He turned toward Holmes. "Has there been an increase of other crime in town? Thefts? Drugs?"

"Some thefts, but that's not unusual. Haven't heard much about drugs being found, though."

Dawson wasn't a cop, but he still thought that was rather unusual. If people were desperate for money, there should be a corresponding rise in other crimes.

"Are you going to put out an arrest warrant for Sean?" Sylvie asked.

"We'll put out a notice to be on the lookout for him, but without evidence of an actual crime, I can't just arrest him. He must have had access to the money, so we can't say he stole it."

"He may not have stollen it, but add the ten grand to the multiple attacks on Sylvie and you have to admit it's suspicious. That should be more than enough for probable cause."

Holmes scowled. "What, are you a cop now? Or a lawyer?"

"No, but you must realize the two issues are related. Talk to the DA," he advised. "I'm sure he'll support an arrest warrant."

"I'll talk to Sheriff Marty Cline first." Holmes tucked the bank information into his pocket. "Anything else happen that I should get on record?"

"We found a campsite two hundred and fifty yards off lizard trail," Dawson said. "Spotted a guy in a red shirt from the chopper, then stumbled across the campsite. We haven't found the trespasser, though."

"If the guy was Sean, he wouldn't be trespassing, would he?" Holmes asked.

"No, he wouldn't. But it's still strange that someone would be camping out there," Sylvie said. "Someone living on the side of the mountain could have done all of these attacks against me."

"What about the shooting in town?" Holmes asked.

"That might be an aberration," Sylvie admitted.

"We've been operating under the assumption that the attacks were the work of one person," Dawson admitted. "But it could be that two men are involved."

Holmes squinted at him for a long moment. "You're thinking that if Sean owes this Ben Stuart money, that he's the one who sicced a couple of guys on Sylvie."

"Exactly." Dawson frowned, thinking that if there was more than one guy out there, he needed to get one of his SEAL teammates out there for backup.

Dallas was his first thought. He and Dallas had been swim buddies going through BUD/S training, and he'd be familiar with ranch life. Dallas had mentioned family issues, but maybe that was resolved by now.

The main problem? Montana was a mighty long car ride from Texas. Other than Alaska, they were the two biggest states. A plane ride would work, but Dillon's airport wouldn't be easily accessed from other big cities. To make it easier for Dallas, he hoped to convince Sylvie to pick him up via chopper in Helena.

"Do you mind if I use your restroom?" Holmes asked, his expression sheepish. "Long drive back to Dillon."

"Sure." Sylvie hesitated, then added, "I haven't mentioned Sean's withdrawals to my father yet. You know he's still getting cancer treatments, and I don't want to worry him."

"I'm just checking in to make sure things are going all right after the barn fire," Holmes said with a wink. "Nothing more."

"Thanks." Sylvie led the way inside.

Dawson stayed outside with Kilo. He pulled out his phone and called Dallas.

"Dawg!" Dallas greeted him by his SEAL nickname. "Long time, man. How are you feeling? No more surgeries on the horizon, I hope."

"I'm fine." He prayed each night that he wouldn't need more surgeries.

"What's happening?"

"I've got a bit of a situation here," Dawson admitted. "I know you've been tied up with family issues too, but my neighbor Sylvie McLane is in danger. And it's looking more like there's a couple of guys out to get her. I could use some backup if you have time. If not, no worries. I'll call one of the other guys."

"You mean the old married men?" Dallas snickered.

"Well, except for Nico. From what I hear, he's still trying to find a line on Ava. I'm starting to worry that all he's going to find is her dead body."

"I know." It was a horrible thought, but you didn't fight terrorists for twenty years without expecting the worst. Nico and Jaydon were swim buddies, and Nico wouldn't stop searching for Jaydon's sister Ava until he found her, dead or alive. "I've offered to help. He said he'll call us in when he needs us."

"Same here," Dallas admitted. "Maybe the old married guys will even help, if they can pry themselves away from their women and kids. Mason and Aubrey are talking about adopting another one to give Lucas a younger brother or sister. And did you hear that Charlotte is pregnant? I'm sure Kendra is next. Not sure what they're thinking having kids at our age. That's a young man's game."

The image of his SEAL teammates chasing kids made him grin. Who would have thought that Mason, Kaleb, and Hudson would all be married within seven months of landing stateside? If he hadn't seen Hudd's lovesick face for himself, he never would have believed it. Or the other guys' besotted expressions for that matter. Between his multiple surgeries, he'd managed to make all three weddings.

Sylvie's face flashed in his mind. It was all too easy to imagine her wearing a wedding dress and holding a bouquet of wildflowers straight from McLane Mountain.

Don't go there, he warned. Putting down roots in Montana wasn't part of his master plan.

"Dawg?" Dallas prompted. "When do you need me? I'll bring Romeo too. He's turned out to be a fine tracker."

Romeo was a chocolate lab, a few months older than Kilo. Dallas had gotten Romeo when they'd all gone to visit Lillian, the woman who made it her mission to provide all military vets dogs of their own. Mason had arranged for their entire team to get dogs, and he had to admit, Kilo had been a good companion after his surgeries.

"Are you sure you can come?" Dawson swallowed a flash of guilt. "I don't want to cause issues with your family."

"Things have calmed down here," Dallas admitted. "I'm sure my leaving for a few days won't hurt. Where are you again? Someplace in Montana?"

"Dillon is the closest town." He noticed Sylvie and Holmes coming back out of the house. Kilo wagged his tail and ran over to greet Sylvie as if she'd been gone for days instead of minutes. "If you can fly into Helena, that's the biggest city here. I'm sure I can borrow my neighbor's chopper to come pick you and Romeo up."

"Okay, give me some time to get a few things settled. I'll try to be there by tomorrow, mid to late afternoon."

"That's fine. Call me when you've made your travel arrangements."

"Will do. Be safe, Dawg. Don't do anything crazy until I get there to cover your six," Dallas said.

"Roger that." He disconnected from the line and crossed over to join Sylvie and Holmes.

"Who was that?" Sylvie asked, her green eyes curious. Then she shrugged. "Sorry, I know it's not any of my business."

"No big secret. That was my buddy Dallas. He and his chocolate lab, Romeo, are going to head out to help. I hope it's okay that I promised to pick him up via the chopper when he arrives in Helena."

"That's fine, we have plenty of room."

He mentally kicked himself for not asking that it was okay to have Dallas and Romeo stay at the ranch house too.

"We'll probably take turns using the guest room so that one of us is always awake and on guard."

She gave him a strange look but simply nodded. "Whatever you think is best, although things have been quiet for a while."

"Don't say the Q word," he warned. Every time someone did that while on a mission, things went sideways real fast.

"Superstitious?" she teased.

"No. God is watching over us. Just saying, the minute you think things have settled down, something new hits."

"He's not wrong," Rick said wryly. His radio crackled, and he lifted the handpiece from his shoulder. "This is Holmes, what's up?"

"Boss, we got a report of a dead body," the dispatcher's voice was loud enough for them to all hear. "Young male pulled out of Beaverhead River."

"Where exactly?" Holmes asked, his expression grim as he darted a glance at Sylvie. Dawson knew he was imagining the dead body was that of Sean McLane.

"The report came in from the RV park. Figure you'd want to head over."

"I'll be there as soon as possible." Holmes clipped the radio back to his collar and turned toward the squad.

"Wait! We're coming with you!" Sylvie shouted.

"This is a police matter," Holmes shot back. "I'll let you know if it's anything related to your case."

Seconds later, Holmes was peeling down the long, winding driveway, red lights and sirens all the way.

"Come on, I'll drive." Dawson knew there was no point in trying to hold Sylvie back. "My SUV so we can take Kilo."

"Thank you." She hurried toward the vehicle.

He didn't have red lights or sirens, but he kept his foot to the floor, following in the deputy's wake. Considering the situation, he figured there wouldn't be any deputies on patrol to pull him over.

"You think it's Sean." Sylvie's soft voice broke the silence.

He was very much afraid it was, but he wasn't going to say that. "Try not to lose hope, Sylvie. It's summertime, for all we know, some tourist got drunk, fell in the river, and drowned."

"Maybe." He could tell she wanted to believe that.

"We're only thinking the worst because of what we learned about illegal gambling going on," he added. "Typically, people who are in debt to loan sharks aren't killed. Dead men don't pay."

"Great. That's reassuring." Her tone indicated otherwise.

He decided it was best to keep his mouth shut. He pushed the speed limit all the way to Dillon while keeping an eye on Kilo in the crate area. The dog didn't seem to mind the high speed.

The Beaverhead campground and RV park was on the west side of town. Dawson headed that way, pulling to a stop where a series of squads were parked. In a flash, Sylvie was out of the car and pushing through the crowd of gawkers.

Muttering under his breath, he took a moment to let Kilo out. He had to use the leash because of all the people. He elbowed his way into the group.

"Sylvie, stay back," Holmes barked. "It's not Sean, okay? It's not Sean!"

"Who is it?" Sylvie demanded.

There was a momentary silence before someone else, not Holmes, called out, "Matt Keagan."

"Everyone back off. This is a crime scene," Holmes shouted irritably.

The group of onlookers moved back several steps. Dawson did too, searching the crowd for Sylvie.

Knowing the dead man was Matt Keagan didn't help much. Last anyone saw Sean, he was with his two buddies Matt and Ned.

Now that Matt was dead, he had to assume either Ned or Sean was culpable.

Or in danger of ending up the same way.

CHAPTER ELEVEN

Her chest was so tight she couldn't breathe.

After pushing through the crowd, she still couldn't see the dead man because of the police and EMTs surrounding the body. And maybe that was for the best.

Someone claimed the dead man wasn't Sean but his friend Matt. She desperately wanted to believe that to be true. Not that anyone ending up dead was good news. Yet despite whatever bad things Sean had done, she couldn't bear the idea of him being dead.

She forced herself to take a deep breath. If Sean was still alive, then where was he? Hiding? Maybe that had been him camping near lizard trail.

Rick came over, waving them back even farther. "Come on now, this is a crime scene. I need you all to stay back."

She met his gaze for a long moment, and he gave a tiny nod as if to reassure her the dead man wasn't Sean. After giving him a look of gratitude, she turned and made her way back to Dawson.

"Hey, are you okay?" Dawson drew her close. Kilo greeted her enthusiastically, and it occurred to her that dogs didn't have bad days. Unless, of course, they had terrible owners, but Kilo was happy all the time.

She wanted to be like Kilo.

"The victim is not Sean, but that isn't necessarily good news, is it?" She allowed herself the luxury of leaning against Dawson. "Sean, Ned, and Matt must have gotten involved in the illegal gambling ring. It's the only thing that makes sense."

"It seems that way, but we'll need to let the deputies do their investigation. At this point, we don't know for sure that Matt was murdered. His death could be accidental."

She remembered the look Holmes had given her. "I have a feeling it wasn't. Rick called the area near the river a crime scene."

"I heard, but that's the usual default response until the scene has been processed. The ME will determine cause of death. Come on, Sylvie. Let's go." Dawson gave her a quick hug. "Nothing more we can do here."

Convinced Sean was the one who'd been camping near the rock, she nodded in agreement. Dawson untangled Kilo's leash but kept her tucked close to his side as they headed back to his SUV. The way Dawson seemed to be watching everyone around them made her realize he was concerned about more gunfire.

He was playing the role of bodyguard, the way he'd promised. Staying alert and expecting danger around every corner. She should be glad he was taking her safety so seriously.

Yet, deep down, she'd rather be on the receiving end of another one of his incredible kisses instead.

"Ready?"

It took her a moment to realize he'd opened her door and was waiting for her to get in. She nodded and slid into the passenger seat. He closed the door, went around back to let Kilo in, then came around to the driver's side.

"We'll need to take another trip up the mountain." She glanced at him as he drove through town. "I'm sure the man in the red shirt was Sean. We need to convince him to come forward and to work with law enforcement."

Dawson didn't say anything for several minutes. When he turned onto the highway that would take them back to her ranch, he broke the silence. "My only goal is to keep you safe, Sylvie. You know as well as I do that Sean is somehow behind these attacks. If not doing them personally, then arranging them." He paused, then added, "I'm leaning toward the idea that Sean and Ned are coordinating together."

"Maybe it's someone else, like the men Sean and Ned owe money to. That guy, Ben Stuart. He could have hired someone." It wasn't a likely scenario, and she knew it. But she didn't want to believe her brother had tried to hurt her.

"Maybe." Dawson's tone held doubt. "But it would still have to be someone familiar with McLane Mountain."

"Yes." Her mind went back to the barn fire and the way the horses were spared. Only a rancher or a ranch hand would think to do that. "Okay, fine. We'll say Sean and Ned are working together. I still want to find Sean. I'm sure I can get him to turn himself in."

"If you wait until tomorrow, my buddy Dallas will help."

"I'm not waiting. We just learned Matt's dead, and for all we know, Sean and Ned are next. I'll pack sandwiches for dinner and hit the trail when we get back."

He sighed loud enough for her to hear him. "I'm not letting you go alone. But I have one request. Can we take the chopper again? That will cut down the amount of time it will take us to get to lizard trail."

She hesitated, then nodded. Personally, she'd rather ride, yet she couldn't argue that it might be better for them to be on foot rather than on horseback. Especially remembering how stealthily Dawson could move through the brush.

Difficult to sneak up on someone via horseback.

"Thanks." Dawson continued looking around as he drove. "I'll feel better when Dallas gets here."

"Your swim buddy."

"Yeah. We've been on the same SEAL team for twenty years. Until that last op . . ." His voice trailed off.

She thought about his multiple surgeries and rested a hand on his forearm. "I'm glad you're here now. Although I feel awful about dragging someone else into my situation." She grimaced. "Bad enough that I've been keeping you away from helping your father run the Copper Creek."

"It's no big deal. My dad and Max have things under control, and trust me, Dallas doesn't mind taking a break from whatever issues he's been dealing with back home." He frowned as he looked in the rearview mirror. "There's a black truck coming up fast."

"What?" She twisted in her seat to look through Kilo's crated area to the stretch of highway behind them. Sure enough, a black truck was steamrolling toward them. "Dawson? I don't think they're planning to stop."

He nodded and surprisingly slowed his speed. She wanted to ask what he was doing, but he abruptly turned off the road, made a circle in the field, then brought the truck to a stop. Kilo slid around in the crate area. She swallowed hard as Dawson pulled his weapon and lowered his window, training it on the truck.

Tires squealed as the truck abruptly slowed. Her heart lodged in her throat when Dawson fired one shot, hitting the rear panel of the truck. There was no way Dawson would miss hitting whatever he was aiming at, so she had to assume he'd targeted the rear panel on purpose.

The passenger side window of the truck went down. The sun was setting in the west, making it difficult to see clearly.

The strong scent of gas wafted toward them. Dawson had hit the gas tank!

"Stay down," Dawson warned as he put the SUV in gear and hit the accelerator. Gunfire echoed from the truck. She covered her head with her hands but didn't hear the metallic sound of their car being hit.

After what seemed like forever, Dawson put his hand on her shoulder. "You can sit up now."

She straightened and turned to peer behind them. The truck was a dot in the distance. "Shouldn't we go back and find out who they were?"

"Only one man, who was armed." Dawson glanced at her. "The glint of the sun made it difficult to get a decent look at the driver's face, but I did see a gun. And I told you before, my priority is to keep you safe."

She hoped and prayed the driver wasn't Sean. Her brother didn't have a black truck, but maybe Ned did. "But . . ."

"No, Sylvie. Going back isn't worth the risk. If I was alone, maybe, but not with you and Kilo along for the ride. You need to call Holmes to let him know about this," Dawson said firmly. "He needs to be on the lookout for a black Ford pickup truck with a bullet hole in the gas tank."

Fumbling for her phone, she nodded. "I—uh, okay. But

he's probably not going to leave the crime scene at Beaver-head River."

"I know." Dawson scowled. "I'm sure that was exactly what the driver of the truck planned on."

She made the call but was forced to leave a message on his voice mail. So she called the general dispatch number. Brenda Eastman picked up the call. "Beaverhead County Sheriff's Department."

"Brenda, this is Sylvie again. Look, I've been working with Deputy Rick Holmes regarding several incidents that have happened recently. There's a black Ford pickup truck that followed us out of town. When we stopped and turned to face off with the driver, he took a shot at us."

"Mercy, Sylvie, that sounds terrible. Who was with you? Your dad?"

"No, ah, Dawson Steele. From the Copper Creek Ranch. Dawson fired back at the truck, hitting the gas tank. Deputy Holmes should be able to find the Ford with a bullet hole in the gas tank, okay? And if he has questions, have him call me or Dawson."

"I will, hun." In the background, she could hear finger-tips hitting the keyboard. She assumed Brenda was sending a message to the deputy about the truck. "I heard Dawson was back in town, is he as hot as everyone is saying?"

"I—um, guess so. Gotta run, thanks, Brenda." She quickly disconnected from the call, fearing Brenda would go on and on about Dawson, who was definitely as hot as everyone was saying. Yet he was also so much more than good-looking.

He was everything Paul Griffin wasn't. Kind, sweet, protective, hardworking, and confident. Years ago, when the news had reached them that he'd become a Navy SEAL, the entire town of Dillon had been full of pride at learning one of their own had become the best of the best.

Seeing Dawson in action over these past few days, she knew he was the best, period. Always cool under fire. Always thinking ahead. Never taking anything for granted.

Raking her fingers through her hair, she tried to calm her racing heart. First Sean's dead friend Matt, then this latest attempt to hurt or kill them.

No, not them. Not Dawson. She was the target.

And the McLane Mountain Ranch was the ultimate reward.

IT BURNED to drive away from the scene of a shooting. If Dallas had been there to protect Sylvie, Dawson would have gone after the driver of the Ford truck without hesitation. Getting his identity, and that of whoever had hired him, would have helped put an end to these ridiculous attacks.

Yet leaving Sylvie and Kilo wasn't an option.

He let out a soundless sigh as he left the highway to take the long, winding driveway to Sylvie's ranch. Dallas would be there tomorrow. Hopefully, they'd come up with a plan to draw this guy and any accomplices out of hiding.

The sooner they could go on offense, the better.

He glanced at Sylvie's pale, drawn features. Hopefully, this latest attempt would change her mind about heading back to the mountain.

"We really need to find Sean," she said as if reading his thoughts. "I know he must have gotten involved in the gambling ring and can't see a way out. I can help him, but only if he does his part to get these thugs behind bars."

He knew without being told Sylvie would bail her brother out financially if needed. Which really is something Sean should know as well. If he wanted out.

"Waiting until tomorrow won't hurt," he said, trying to buy time.

"I'm not waiting." Her tone was curt. "By tomorrow, Sean could be found dead in the Beaverhead River. Or the Copper Creek."

"Okay, fine." He tried not to sound as annoyed as he felt. "We'll stick to the original plan of using the chopper to get to the lizard trail, then hike up the mountain from there." He thought about it for a moment. "I think we'll take Kilo with us this time."

"Are you sure?"

No, he wasn't sure about this idea at all. But he wanted to have every possible advantage, and that meant bringing Kilo. He looked at the lab using the rearview mirror. Thankfully, the canine didn't look troubled by the way he'd skidded around the crate area when Dawson had been forced to go off-road. The dog was resilient, that was for sure.

He stopped the SUV in front of the ranch house. The hour wasn't that late, only two-thirty in the afternoon, but it seemed later. Maybe because they'd been going nonstop since that morning.

The only easy day was yesterday, he reminded himself. It was the SEAL mantra. Every single op they'd ever gone on they'd prepared for the worst.

Their last op had been the worst of all.

"I'll make sandwiches for the trail," Sylvie said. "We'll need to make sure we have enough food and water, especially if we find him. Oh, and we have extra cowboy hats too. The sun will be brutal up there."

"Okay." He could appreciate she was thinking positive, it was what they'd often done during deployments. Yet finding Sean on the massive ranch would not be easy. Unless, of course, he wanted to be found.

Dawson packed Kilo's collapsible food and water dishes, along with at least two servings of food. He stuffed them into a backpack that he normally carried in the SUV. Then he went back out to the vehicle, rummaging around until he found a length of coiled rope.

He holstered his weapon, added extra ammo, and double-checked his knife. Unable to think of anything else critical to take, he headed back inside.

"Ready?" Sylvie asked. She handed him a brown cowboy hat, wearing a similar one on her head. He frowned when he noticed she had a thick backpack over her shoulder too. He almost offered to carry it for her, then stopped himself. This trip was her idea. He needed to trust she could carry her own weight.

And if she couldn't? Then he'd take it for her.

"Yep." He managed a smile as he settled the hat on his head. She was right about the sun. "Let's go."

Outside the chopper hangar, they went through the same routine as earlier that morning. First dragging the bird outside, then going through the preflight checklist. It seemed like eons ago that they'd gone up and caught a glimpse of the man wearing a red shirt. Personally, he felt this would be a useless trip, but he kept his thoughts to himself.

After storing his pack and Sylvie's in the back, he gestured for Kilo to jump up into the bird. He made sure there was an extra pair of headphones for the canine to protect his hearing from the loud engine.

Ten minutes later, they were airborne. He'd taken the

stick again because Sylvie wanted to search the countryside for signs of her brother.

"I can't believe Kilo is wearing headphones," she said as he banked toward the north ridge. "He's like a little human sometimes."

"He's a good companion, that's for sure." Dawson glanced at Kilo, smiling at the image the dog made sitting behind them wearing headphones. He and Sylvie had exchanged their cowboy hats for headphones too. The dog seemed at home in the chopper, and he made a mental note to start up Kilo's training sessions again. The yellow lab would be an excellent tracker if given the chance.

He repeated the same route they'd taken that morning, passing the mountain ridge one way, then banking around to do another sweep. Sylvie had her face pressed against the window but didn't indicate she saw anything.

"Let me know when you're ready for me to set her down," he said.

"One more pass," she responded. "Then we'll land."

Worked for him. He repeated the curve and went past both the west and north mountains. Then he slowly lowered the bird to the ground in the same location they'd used earlier.

After shutting down the engine, he reached over to remove Kilo's headphones. The dog shook his head back and forth as if glad to be rid of them.

He jumped down, smiling when the dog followed his lead. Grabbing both backpacks, he handed the lighter one to Sylvie. After donning their hats, they took a moment to add a couple of water bottles to each pack, then turned toward the mountain.

"You want to go back up the lizard trail?" he asked.

She took a moment to look around. "Yes, for now. This

time, though, let's go to the east side of the trail toward the small cave Sean and I found as kids."

"Okay, lead the way." He shouldered the pack and gave Kilo the hand signal to come.

Sylvie headed up the trail without hesitation. Kilo surged forward, leaving Dawson to cover their backs, the way he liked it.

They hiked for a solid twenty minutes before she stopped to rest. He had to admire her unflagging energy. Ignoring the pain radiating from his abdominal muscles, he drank from one of the water bottles, then filled Kilo's collapsible bowl.

"At the next curve in the trail, we're going to head east," she told him. "There's another much smaller trail that branches off from this one. It will take us all the way to the cave."

He nodded. "Sounds good." He wanted to ask what the plan would be if the cave was empty but decided to keep quiet. This was her mission; he was just there to offer his support and protection.

After storing Kilo's bowl in his pack, they continued winding their way up the trail. The mountainside was beautiful, but he only gave it a passing thought. His gaze lingered on any hidden spot an assailant might be lying in wait.

There were far too many possibilities for his peace of mind.

Kilo didn't notice anything amiss, which helped. Once they left the lizard trail, the terrain became more difficult. Too many rocks, trees, debris, and thick brush to make moving silently an option.

So different from the desert of Afghanistan. And from the California coast.

Another fifteen minutes passed before Sylvie took

another break. Sweat dampened her temples beneath the brim of her hat and stained her T-shirt. He was sure he looked far worse.

"See that open spot between the two large trees?" She gestured to the east side of their location. "That's roughly where the cave is located."

"Will you stay here while I check it out?" To his eye, it seemed the perfect place for an ambush.

"No way. I'm going up first." She lifted her chin, her gaze narrowing as she met his gaze. "If Sean is up there, he'll talk to me."

Maybe, maybe not. He wasn't as convinced as she was that her younger brother happened to get in over his head. For all they knew, he was working directly with Ben Stuart. "How about if we both go, but you allow me to take the lead? It's better to be safe if someone else is hiding up there."

She hesitated, then finally nodded. "That's fine."

"Good." He shrugged into his pack and stepped around her on the mostly invisible trail. He scanned the area for a moment, looking for the best approach. Going straight up to the cave opening was not happening. They'd approach from the side to minimize the danger.

The terrain was steep, and he had to use the nearby trees and brush to help steady himself. When he reached the trees she'd mentioned earlier, he stopped and went down on his knees. Partially to catch his breath, but more so to check the area for signs that a human had been there.

Kilo sat beside him. He panted in the way dogs did to cool themselves down.

"See anything?" Sylvie whispered.

He shook his head. "We'll stay to the west side, understand?"

"Got it." He was glad she didn't argue.

After a brief rest, he set out again, taking a wide arc to approach the cave. He was surprised when they reached the spot without incident.

"Sean?" Sylvie called loudly. "Are you in there?"

There was no response.

"Sean, this is serious. You have to come out. Matt is dead. Do you hear me? Matt is dead!"

He inwardly winced. That wasn't the way he'd have approached it, but the continued silence seemed to indicate there was no one inside.

"Give me a minute to check it out." He slid the pack off his shoulders, setting it lightly on the ground. "I promise not to do anything rash."

She sighed. "Okay, fine."

"Kilo, stay." The dog sat, his ears perked forward. Sylvie knelt beside the lab, holding on to his collar. Dawson moved toward the cave opening, slipping the Sig Sauer from its holster. He'd promised not to do anything rash, but he fully intended to protect himself and Sylvie from any attack.

Even one from her brother.

He sidled up to the cave entrance, listening intently. Still nothing. He went down to his knee again, then peered around the edge.

The area just inside the cave appeared empty. Moving cautiously, he went farther inside.

It took a moment for his gaze to adjust to the dim light. Instantly he noticed another firepit, similar to the one near the protruding rock.

He quickly crossed over and put his hand over the darkened remains. They were cold to the touch, but that didn't mean someone hadn't recently spent the night. Maybe this had been the original location used by the guy in the red shirt.

"Dawson?" Sylvie whispered.

He stood and went all the way to the back of the cave. It wasn't very deep, but a large rocky wall indicated it may have been a former copper mine with a tunnel that had collapsed.

Finding nothing, he returned to the cave opening. "No one is here now." He gestured for her to come inside.

She swept past him, her gaze landing on the firepit. "I'm sure Sean was here."

"Yeah, but when? The embers are cold. Could have been left yesterday, a week ago, or a year ago." He holstered his weapon. "We'll rest here for a bit before heading back down to the chopper."

She dropped to sit with her back propped against the wall and reached into the pack. "We can rest, but there's still plenty of daylight. We can keep looking a while longer."

He idly rubbed his abdominal muscles. "You have another possible location in mind? Because if not, there's no point in trudging through the wilderness."

She didn't answer right away. Kilo stretched out near his feet, his nose pointed toward the cave opening. "No, I don't have another idea on where to look," she finally admitted. "But I don't want to head back to the ranch yet."

He tried not to groan out loud. He didn't want to hold her back, but he didn't like the idea of wandering around the mountain either. He figured he'd give her another hour, then call it quits.

"Should we eat now or later?" Sylvie asked.

"Later." He moved toward the cave opening. "The sun will be behind the mountains soon. Best to make use of the full daylight while we can."

"Okay." She stuffed the water bottle back inside her pack and stood. She joined him at the cave opening. "Let's head farther east."

"Fine with me." Before he could move, a crack of gunfire echoed loudly. He roughly lunged sideways, dragging Sylvie down and covering Kilo the best he could. "Back into the cave," he hissed.

She nodded and scrambled back. He pushed Kilo that way, then followed.

Being trapped in the cave by the gunman hadn't been a scenario he'd anticipated.

A mistake that could prove fatal.

CHAPTER TWELVE

The gunfire didn't make sense. Sylvie knew the guy in the truck who'd shot at them was still miles away. He'd have had to wait for a tow truck or get picked up by a friend and abandon the damaged Ford. Either way, there's no way the same guy could have gotten to the mountainside this quickly.

Sean? A helpless fury washed over her. What was wrong with her brother? These nonstop attacks were getting old.

"I need you to stay here with Kilo while I see if I can get out of the cave without the gunman seeing me."

"Wait." She grabbed his arm. "I don't think that's a good idea. If he has a rifle, he likely has a scope."

His blue eyes bored into hers. "I'm not going to sit here doing nothing."

She held his gaze, knowing it was her fault that they were in this predicament. "I'm sorry, Dawson. I guess this was a bad idea."

"It's my fault for not anticipating this possibility." He

sighed and turned to look through the cave opening. "The good news is the sun is going down. At some point, it will be too dark for the gunman to see us clearly."

Trying to get down the mountain in the dark would be difficult at best. Between the hazardous trail and the wildlife, their chances of getting safely down to the chopper were not good.

"Okay, if we have to move at dark, there's no reason for you to head out now." She didn't release his arm. "Please, Dawson. Don't do this."

He lightly covered her hand with his. "It's a simple recon mission. I won't go far. But consider this, which direction did the shot come from? We're halfway up the north ridge, the only possibility is that he's stationed along the western mountainside."

She stared down at their joined hands for a long moment. "You're right. It would be difficult to shoot at a target standing just outside the cave entrance from higher up on the north ridge. The angle doesn't work. Same thing for being down below. He must be sitting somewhere west of here." She frowned, thinking about possible locations, which were too many to count. "That's a long-distance shot."

"Might be why he missed." Dawson gently squeezed her hand, then pulled out of her grasp. "I won't go far. Just give me a few minutes, okay?"

She knew he would go, no matter what she said. "Okay."

He rubbed Kilo's fur, then stood. He made his way to the cave entrance, staying toward the side closest to where they estimated the shooter to be. It also happened to be where a large tree could be used as cover.

One second he was standing there, the next he was gone. She swallowed hard, reminding herself that Dawson knew more about moving stealthily through the brush than anyone she'd ever known. His training would serve him well.

Looping her arm around Kilo's neck, she cuddled the lab, for her sake more than his. "He'll be back soon, Kilo."

The lab licked her ear, making her smile. Amazing, really, considering she was stuck in a cave while Dawson risked his life to find the gunman. Guilt plagued her. She felt so certain she'd find Sean, convincing him to go with her to the police.

Instead, she'd put Dawson's life on the line. Again.

She lifted her heart in prayer and whispered, "Lord, please keep Dawson safe." On some level, she was surprised at how she turned to prayer. Dawson's influence for sure.

She strained to listen but heard nothing. No additional gunfire after that initial shot. That had to be good news, right? Maybe the gunman had taken off.

Her stomach rumbled with hunger, but she didn't open her pack for the sandwiches she'd packed. She wouldn't eat until Dawson returned.

Kilo kept going toward the cave opening, no doubt searching for his owner. She brought him back several times. Finally, she hauled the sixty-plus-pound canine onto her lap and stroked his fur until he fell asleep.

One problem solved. If only the rest of her tenuous situation could be fixed so easily.

After twenty minutes had passed, Dawson stepped back into the cave. Kilo awoke from his nap, leaped off her lap, and ran over to greet him. "He missed you," she murmured.

"I see that." He bent to lavish attention on the dog, then came over to sit beside her. "The bad news is that I didn't find anything. The good news is that there haven't been any more shots fired."

"You think the gunman is gone?"

"I think it's possible he's on the move." Dawson offered a tired smile. "We'll stay hidden for a while yet. When the sun goes down, we'll head back down the mountain."

"I'm on board with sitting here for a while." She glanced around the cave, wishing for a pair of sleeping bags. "It's going to be treacherous heading down in the dark. We can always stay here until morning."

"I considered that, but the guy might anticipate that and hang around too. I think it's a risk we'll have to take."

If anyone could accomplish such a feat, it was Dawson. She nodded, then pulled her backpack over. "Time to eat."

He put a hand over his abdomen. "You can hear my stomach growling?"

"No, that's my stomach," she teased, lightly bumping her shoulder against his. Dawson wasn't just an amazing protector, but he was fun to be with. This camaraderie between them was something she'd never had before. Certainly not with Paul. She pulled two thick turkey sandwiches from her pack and handed him the larger one. Then she took out two water bottles too. "Here you go."

"Thanks." He set the sandwich down, giving Kilo a narrow look when the dog sniffed at it, then reached for her hand. "Dear Lord, we thank You for keeping us safe in Your care. We ask for Your blessing and guidance as we seek those responsible for hurting others. Amen."

"Amen." She clung to his hand for a moment before letting go. "I'm really sorry about dragging you here. We should have just stayed at the ranch."

"Don't worry about it." He leaned over to kiss her cheek. Despite the seriousness of the situation, she wished he'd kiss her properly. The way he had before. "I don't have a brother, but if one of my SEAL teammates was suspected of doing something wrong, I'd still risk my life to protect them."

His sentiment was sweet, but she was beginning to believe Sean didn't deserve it. Whatever her brother had gotten himself involved with, he'd done of his own free will. No one forced him to gamble. Or to come after her. If Sean had just continued working the ranch, the way they had growing up, none of this would be happening.

Depressed by the thought, her appetite vanished. Still, she forced herself to eat. She'd need all the strength and smarts she had to get them down the side of the mountain to reach the chopper.

When they finished eating, Dawson filled the two collapsible bowls with kibble and water for Kilo. The dog eagerly chowed his food. When the sun had dipped low enough behind the western mountain ridge, Dawson stood and shrugged into his pack.

"Time to go."

She nodded and looped her arms through her backpack. It was lighter now that they'd consumed the water and sandwiches. She'd kept a few PowerBars hidden inside just in case they were forced to spend the night.

Strange, but the idea of staying here all night with Dawson didn't bother her. In fact, she might be just a bit disappointed that his goal was to head down the mountain.

"I'll go first," Dawson said. "You stay behind me as much as possible. If you hear gunfire, hit the ground."

"I will." Arguing with him would be fruitless. Besides, by now he was becoming familiar with the trails. She trusted his sense of direction would get them down to the helicopter.

They walked in silence as the last rays of sunshine slid behind the mountain peak. There was still some ambient light, but that would fade fast. Several times her foot slipped on a rock or fallen debris, but she managed to stay upright.

Watching Kilo helped, his yellow fur visible against the dark ground. She learned to lift her feet higher when he did, avoiding some of the debris. They were not moving very fast, and she estimated it would take them almost as long to get down as it had to climb up.

Dawson lifted a hand. She froze as he scanned the area around them. Was it possible the gunman had tracked their movements through the scope, despite the encroaching darkness? If the gunman was Sean, he may have assumed she'd go to the cave and could attempt to intercept them on the most logical path down the mountain.

Her brother wasn't the tracker Dawson was, though, so she felt certain Dawson must have heard him approach. They stood in the darkness for several long moments before Dawson made a gesture with his hand indicating they could keep going.

Kilo sniffed along the trail as they went. No doubt the canine would alert them if any wild animals approached. Hopefully, they didn't cross paths with a bear, bobcat, moose, or wolf. All animals she'd glimpsed in the woods while riding over the years. Scary to imagine Kilo trying to defend them against something that dangerous. And she knew the dog would attempt to do just that.

They hiked for another fifteen minutes. She stepped on a rock, twisting her ankle. A soft cry escaped her lips, and Dawson quickly whirled around. "What happened?" he whispered.

"Twisted my ankle." She bent down to massage it. "I'll be okay, just give me a minute."

Dawson came back up the trail to kneel beside her. He gently palpated the joint, then grimaced. "We may need to head back to the cave."

"No, I can walk." She didn't want to hold them up. "It's fine, truly."

"Hold on. I have a wrap in here that will offer support." He slid off his backpack and poked around inside. When he found the wrap, he eased her left foot from the hiking boot and expertly applied the elastic support.

"Thanks." She quickly put the boot back on before her ankle swelled to the point that was impossible.

"Don't thank me," he said in a low voice full of self-reproach. "It's my fault you were hurt. You were right. We should have spent the night in the cave."

"I'm the one who didn't see the rock." She stood, hiding a wince. "See? I'm fine."

"Nice try. We'll head back to the cave. I don't want to risk anything more happening to you." Dawson rubbed the back of his neck. "We'll head out early in the morning instead."

She felt bad for holding him back. If Dawson and Kilo had been by themselves, she knew they'd make it down the mountain without a problem.

Yet she hated to admit how her injured ankle was beginning to throb in pain. She worried she might fall again if she didn't rest it. "Okay, we'll return to the cave."

Dawson led the way back up the mountainside. It didn't take that long as they hadn't made it very far. She gratefully sank to the ground, relieving the pressure on her ankle.

"I have a cold pack." Once again he rummaged in his

backpack. Soon he cracked the cold compress seal, then wrapped it around her ankle.

"Thanks." She took off her cowboy hat and rested her head against the cave wall.

After a few minutes, she knew she couldn't ignore the pressure in her bladder for much longer. "I—uh, need to head into the bushes."

He nodded, understanding her need. "You want help?"

"No." Her eyes widened in horror. "This is bad enough as it is."

"Natural," he corrected. "Perfectly natural, Sylvie. I'll take a turn when you're finished."

She had to give him credit for being so professional. The cold pack had helped a bit, but she still hobbled as she made her way back outside.

A few minutes later, she returned, feeling much better. He headed out, taking Kilo with him. She could hear him telling the dog to get busy, assuming that was the animal's cue to do his business. She lowered herself to the ground again, stretching out her legs.

Dawson came over to sit next to her. Then he lifted her up so that she was sitting in front of him. He wrapped his arms around her and whispered in her ear. "Try to get some sleep."

She almost laughed at the idea of sleeping but found herself relaxing against him, soaking up his warmth. Resting her head against his chest was nice. Kilo snuggled up alongside them, making her smile.

As she drifted off to sleep, she secretly wished Dawson would stay by her side forever.

MENTALLY KICKING himself for being so stupid as to risk Sylvie's life by heading down the mountain, he held her close, silently praying her injury wasn't too serious. She was a capable woman, more so than anyone else he'd ever known, but he shouldn't have treated her like one of his SEAL teammates.

She'd said the trail would be treacherous. He should have listened. Yet he didn't like being holed up here, where the gunman had last seen them. If he were the hunter, it would be the first place he'd look. And he wouldn't let the darkness stop him.

Sylvie's breathing slowed as she relaxed fully against him. He lightly kissed the top of her head, thankful she was able to get some rest. Maybe the ankle injury wouldn't hold them back for long. Hopefully, she'd feel better by morning.

The mountainside was too steep for him to carry her down. If she couldn't walk, he'd make a sling for her. Kilo would help him pull her down the trail.

But it wouldn't be a comfortable ride. She'd feel every pinecone, rock, and branch along the way, so he planned to use that method as a last resort.

He dozed a bit, jerking awake at the slightest noise. Gently easing Sylvie to her side, he stood and made his way over to the cave opening.

Kilo opened one eye, peering at him, only to close it again. Apparently, the lab was exhausted.

The night was alive with sounds, but none belonging to a human. There was the screech of a bobcat in the distance, thankfully not too close. There were rustling sounds of other nocturnal creatures, but he didn't see or hear anything too alarming.

Reassured, he returned to where Sylvie was curled on

her side. He stretched out beside her, looping his arm around her waist.

"Dawson?" she murmured.

"I'm here." He tugged her closer.

"I'm glad . . ." Her voice trailed off.

He stared into the darkness for a long moment. Sylvie was getting to him, in a way no woman ever had. He tried not to dwell on what that might mean since he had enough to worry about. Surviving the night, then getting down the mountain without the gunman trying to use them for target practice.

He didn't sleep deeply, but he managed to get enough rest. More than he'd gotten on most of his missions, that was for sure. When he noticed the sliver of dawn lightening the sky, he gently shook Sylvie awake.

"Dawson?" Her sleepy tone made him grin.

"Good morning, it's time to hit the trail." His smile faded. "If your ankle is up to it."

"Only one way to find out." She pushed up into a sitting position, dragging her hand through her hair. "I can't believe I slept." Her gaze found his. "Somehow, I think you didn't."

"I'm fine." It wasn't the first time he'd spent the night with his senses on alert. "Let's check out that ankle."

She bent over and palpated her joint. "It's a bit swollen, but it could be worse."

He felt the joint for himself. "It's not as bad as I feared." He held out his hand. "Stand up, I want to see you walk."

She took his hand, allowing him to tug her upright. She took one step and another. "Honestly, it's better than yesterday. I'm sure I can walk down the mountain to the chopper without a problem."

He wanted to believe her. He took her hands in his and

forced her to look him in the eye. "I need you to be sure, Sylvie. I can always make a sling and get Kilo's help to pull you down the mountain."

"I'm sure." She didn't hesitate. "I won't hold you back any more than I already have."

"You're not holding me back, we're a team." He fought the urge to kiss her. "I would have done the same thing if Dallas or one of the other guys had gotten injured."

Her green eyes were skeptical, but she only gestured to her pack. "I have a couple of protein bars in there. We can have them for breakfast."

"Great, thanks. I need a few minutes to feed Kilo anyway."

Ten minutes later, after eating and taking turns in the nearby bushes, they were ready to go. Kilo was his usual energetic self, which was a good sign. He didn't want to cause his K9 partner any harm.

The eastern sun was already starting to rise, which made him a little nervous. It would be full light far too soon.

He led the way, using as much tree cover as possible as they wound toward the trail. He had to assume the guy was still out there, using his rifle scope to keep an eye on the cave opening.

Thankfully, the trail was easier to navigate, enabling them to make better time. He was reassured when they reached the same point where Sylvie had twisted her ankle in less than half the time.

"Sylvie, are you doing okay?" He gave Kilo the hand signal to sit. "How's your ankle?"

"I'm fine, I'll let you know if that changes. Meanwhile, we keep going."

"Okay. I'll trust your judgment." He turned to continue down the trail.

They made good time, although the sun rose quickly, brightening the area around them. If the gunman was out there, they were easy targets. The only good news was that if the shooter was in the west, the morning sunrise would blind him. He raked his gaze around the area, searching for the telltale glint of light bouncing off the lens of his rifle scope.

He didn't dare pick up the pace though, unwilling to risk potential tendon damage to Sylvie's ankle. The longer they went without hearing gunfire, the more convinced he became that they'd manage to get out of there unscathed.

Praying helped.

They were two-thirds of the way down when he caught a flash of something out of the corner of his right eye. "Get down," he shouted, going to his knees. Kilo ran over to lick him, but his gaze was focused on Sylvie.

She dropped like a stone. "What is it?"

"I don't know." He stared toward the western ridge. Had he caught a glimpse of the shooter? Or had the flash been nothing more than light filtering through some trees?

He took a long time scouring the landscape, trying to find whatever had caught his attention.

But found nothing.

"Dawson?"

He shrugged and slowly stood. "Let's keep pushing forward."

"We're getting close," she said encouragingly. "I can see the chopper sitting exactly where we left it."

"I know." He hoped and prayed the bird hadn't been tampered with. He resumed his progress down the path, keeping Kilo and Sylvie behind him.

Finally, the chopper loomed before them. He glanced back at Sylvie, frowning when he noticed she was limping.

"You told me you were okay," he chided, sliding an arm around her waist.

"I am, look, we made it." Relief tinged her voice.

He supported her weight as they closed the fifty-yard gap between their location and the helicopter. Sylvie gripped him tightly until they reached the helicopter. Then she gratefully rested against the bird.

"We need to do an in-depth preflight check," Dawson said. He bent and gave Kilo some water in his collapsible bowl.

"I know. I thought of the possibility of it being tampered with while we were holed up in the cave." Sylvie rested another moment before pushing away. "Let's do it."

They didn't rush but painstakingly checked everything on the chopper, nose to tail, whirlybirds to the under-carriage.

He even took a sample of fuel from the tank to make sure sand, sugar, or salt hadn't been added.

"What do you think?" Sylvie asked. "I don't see anything out of the ordinary, do you?"

"No, it looks good." He looked again toward the west, searching for the glint he'd caught earlier.

Still nothing.

"Okay, let's get inside." He opened the door, then put both hands around Sylvie's waist to lift her inside. "I'm going to pilot us out of here, okay?"

"Don't get used to this," she teased. "The chopper still belongs to McLane Mountain, not Copper Creek."

"We don't need one." He flashed a cheeky grin. "Our neighbors are nice enough to let us borrow theirs."

"Ha, very funny." She smiled while donning her headset.

"Get up," he told Kilo. The yellow lab leaped into the

chopper, sitting calmly while he put headphones over the dog's ears.

"I still can't believe he tolerates them," Sylvie said wryly.

"Me either. He's a good boy." Dawson settled into the pilot's seat and fired up the engine. The blades overhead began to rotate, slowly at first, then building up speed.

He swept his gaze over the instrument panel, then lifted the bird off the ground. He banked the chopper, heading toward Sylvie's ranch.

The bird shuddered beneath his fingers. He hadn't heard gunfire, the sound of the engine was too loud, but the way the chopper listed to the side made him realize they were hit. On some level, he realized the gunman had bided his time, waiting for them to get airborne before taking his shot.

"Dawson, we're hit!" Sylvie cried.

"I know, hang on." He fought to keep the bird in the air long enough to put some distance between them and the shooter. He scoured the ground below them, searching for a good spot to land. He didn't want to cause the cattle to stampede, but he also didn't want to be too close to the mountainside.

The engine began to misfire. The bird was leaning so far to one side he feared he wouldn't be able to make an emergency landing. Silently praying for God to protect them, he lowered the helicopter down.

Sylvie's side of the chopper hit the ground first. He quickly shut down the engine, causing the bird to bounce off the ground, settling back down with a jarring thump.

He ripped off his headset, then reached back to do the same with Kilo. "Get out and take cover."

Sylvie jumped down from her seat, then scrambled beneath the chopper. He and Kilo quickly joined her.

They were safe for the moment, but not for long. He needed to get Sylvie out of there.

Too bad, he was fast running out of ideas on how to accomplish his mission.

CHAPTER THIRTEEN

Ignoring her throbbing ankle, Sylvie took stock of their situation. They were in the west pasture, one of the farthest from the ranch house.

"Do you have binocs in the bird?" Dawson asked.

"Yes. Do you want me to grab them?"

"No, stay here. I'll do it." He slid out from beneath the chopper, using the bird for cover, and quickly rummaged inside. He returned in what seemed like record time with the small binocs. He lifted them to his eyes. "Much better."

That was only part of the problem. What they really needed was a way out. She squirmed around until she could pull her phone from her pocket. "I'll call Josh, ask him to head over to get us out of here."

Dawson nodded, his gaze working constantly as he alternately used the binocs to survey the area. They couldn't see much of the mountain from beneath the bird. She realized he was worried the shooter would come down to ground level to finish the job.

Unfortunately, her call to Josh went straight to voice mail. She ground her teeth and debated calling her father.

She didn't want him to worry, but they needed to get out of there and soon.

Before more gunfire rang out.

"Hi, Sylvie," her dad answered. "Where are you? I didn't see you last night."

"Yeah, I ended up camping in the old cave, but hey, can you find Josh or one of the other ranch hands? The chopper is down, and I need a hand."

"What happened to the chopper?" A hint of concern tainted his tone. "You didn't crash land it, did you?"

Not me, she thought, glancing over at Dawson. "No, but can you find Josh please?"

"Yeah, I'll head to the bunkhouse. See who's around. Call you back." Before she could protest, he disconnected from the call.

The hour was early enough that someone should still be around. She was surprised Josh hadn't answered and told herself it wasn't because he was hiding up on the mountain shooting at them.

The gunman had to be Sean. It was the only thing that made sense. This latest attempt was the most serious yet. If not for Dawson's skill at the stick, they might have been badly injured.

Or dead.

Her phone rang, and she relaxed when she saw Josh's name on the screen. "Josh, we need your help."

"Yeah, I just spoke to your dad. Sorry, I was working and didn't hear my phone." Was it her imagination or did he sound annoyed? She tried to take comfort in knowing Josh wasn't the one trying to hurt her. "What's wrong with the chopper?"

"Someone shot at us, we made an emergency landing, broke one of the landing struts. We're in the west pasture, I need you and a few of the guys to head out on the ATVs to come get us."

"Shot at?" Now he sounded alarmed. "By who?"

Wasn't that the million-dollar question? "I don't know, but I assume the same guy who's been making all these attempts against me."

"Let me talk to him." Dawson lowered the binocs and reached for the phone. "Josh? I want several horseback riders surrounding the ATVs as we ride back to the ranch. We cannot let the shooter make another attempt on Sylvie."

She was close enough to hear Josh's response. "Yeah, good point. I'll have two guys riding two ATVs. I'll bring another couple guys on horseback. We'll keep her surrounded and protected all the way back to the ranch."

"Good." Dawson handed the phone back to her.

"Thanks, Josh." She disconnected from the call and looked at Dawson. "You really think this will work?"

"I'm hoping so."

She settled down to wait. It would take some time for Josh and the others to cross more than half of the fifteen hundred acres of land. After a prolonged silence, she reached over to put a hand on Dawson's arm. "Do you see anything?"

"Not yet." His tone was grim. He absently patted Kilo who was surprisingly calm beneath the bird. "But if it were me, I'd be making my way down to the chopper."

Exactly as she'd thought. "You're armed, right?"

"Yes, ma'am." A hint of humor lightened his tone. "And you can be sure I'll make my jack."

Again with the old west phrases. A reluctant smile lifted a corner of her mouth. She didn't doubt Dawson's ability one bit. His Navy SEAL skills had been proven effective again and again.

She was alive today solely because of him.

Deep down, though, she struggled with the idea of him shooting her brother. Even after everything Sean had done, she couldn't imagine losing him for good.

Spending the next ten to twenty years of his life in prison? Oh yeah, that's what he deserved.

Dead? The possibility made her feel sick.

She didn't say anything to Dawson, though. For one thing, she felt certain he'd shoot as a last resort.

And for another? She knew he'd do whatever he considered necessary to save her life. Even if that meant shooting her brother.

She found herself praying it wouldn't come to that.

The rumble of ATV engines echoed in the distance. From their position under the chopper, she couldn't see anyone approaching, but she was heartened by the sound. Her ranch hands were on the way to rescue them.

Now that she knew they'd survive this latest trial, she grew angry. Bad enough they'd been forced to stay in the cave all night, but damaging the chopper? Who knew how long it would take for her to get it repaired?

"Easy, Kilo," Dawson murmured.

She'd been so immersed in her turbulent thoughts that she hadn't noticed the dog whining. She scooted over to give him more room. "What's bothering him?"

"I'm not sure," Dawson admitted. "But he doesn't normally do this."

She swallowed against a lump of fear. "Does he hear the shooter?"

Dawson didn't answer, but the way he gazed intently toward the mountainside provided the answer. She stiffened, realizing the shooter could get to them before Josh and the ranch hands arrived.

Maybe they weren't safe.

Maybe they'd never be safe.

No, don't give up hope. The thought flashed in her mind, almost as if someone had spoken the words in her ear. She belly-crawled closer to the edge of the chopper so she could search for signs of movement too.

"He's out there somewhere," Dawson muttered. "Come on, you coward. We're here, come and get us."

She swallowed hard, half expecting Sean to do just that. He didn't.

Slowly but surely the sounds of the ATV engines grew louder. Soon she could see a cloud of dust kicked up by the horses and four-wheelers heading toward them. She moved to crawl out from beneath the bird, but Dawson stopped her.

"Me first. Then Kilo, then you."

She nodded, realizing there was no point in arguing. She flexed and extended her left foot, somewhat relieved that lying beneath the helicopter for the past forty-five minutes had helped rest her ankle.

One less problem to deal with in the face of so many others.

"We're over here," Dawson called.

Less than five minutes later, the horseback riders and ATVs arrived. Dawson urged Kilo out, then gestured to Sylvie. "It's safe now."

She crawled out and went up on her hands and knees. Dawson helped her stand. Then he walked her to the closest ATV. Her ankle held up better than she'd dared hope. "Get inside."

Once she was settled, Dawson gestured for the driver to get on the other ATV. "I've got this one."

Ace Abbott frowned and protested. "I can drive her back."

"So can I." Dawson's tone left no room for argument.

Ace glanced at Josh who gave a slight nod, then sullenly moved over to ride with the other ATV driver. Josh and Storm took the lead, the other ranch hands sandwiched them on either side. The second ATV followed behind, eating their dust.

Sylvie didn't breathe normally until they were back at the ranch. She climbed out of the four-wheeler and hobbled into the house. Dawson and Kilo followed. For a moment, she simply stood there, grateful to be home.

"Are you calling Deputy Holmes?" Dawson asked.

"After breakfast." She made a pot of coffee, then opened the fridge and stared blankly inside. Her earlier hunger seemed to have vanished. Maybe she was still a bit shell-shocked from the events that had transpired last night and carried over until this morning.

Dawson nudged her aside. "Sit down. I'll cook while you contact the Beaverhead Sheriff's Department. I'm sure they'll want to see the chopper, especially since it's highly likely there's a bullet lodged inside." He glanced at her over his shoulder. "Are you hungry for anything in particular?"

"Whatever you want is fine." She sank into a kitchen chair, trying not to give into a wave of depression as she made the call. Rick sounded harried but promised to head out as soon as possible. She could tell he was frustrated with these attacks too.

But not as much as she was.

She rubbed Kilo's head as he rested his chin on her knee.

When would it end?

DAWSON HATED SEEING the helplessness etched on Sylvie's features. It was only through God's grace that they were still alive, but the danger was far from over.

He reminded himself that Dallas would be there later that day. Maybe then they could find a way to go on the offensive. Maybe even set a trap.

Without using Sylvie as bait.

He poured them both mugs of coffee, sipping his gratefully before starting breakfast. He whipped up a basic meal of eggs and toast, his mind trying to come up with a way to draw the shooter out of hiding. He and Dallas would need a place to use, a place where Dallas could hide out ahead of time while Dawson drew out the shooter.

Using the same cave they'd stayed in last night was a possibility, although would Sean really believe Sylvie would return to that location? Maybe if there was a way to get a message to him.

He filled two plates with food and joined Sylvie at the table. Then he brought his coffee over too. Reaching across the table, he took her hand in his. "Lord, we humbly thank You for keeping us safe over the past twelve hours and ask that You continue to guide us on the path of truth. Amen."

"Amen." Sylvie offered a lopsided smile. "I prayed for us several times over night and this morning. I have to admit, it seems as if God is truly watching over us."

"He is," Dawson assured her.

For long moments they remained silent, enjoying the food. He was surprised the hour was still early, barely nine in the morning.

It seemed like it should be later. The lack of sleep was

kept at bay thanks to the kick of caffeine. He scrubbed at his stubbled jaw, wishing for a shave and a shower.

"We'll clean up after breakfast," Sylvie said, taking note of his action. "We probably should have done that first."

"Nah, I was hungry." He eagerly took another bite of his eggs. "I'm surprised your father isn't here."

Her brow furrowed. "Yeah, I would have thought he'd be here asking questions about the chopper too." She abruptly jumped to her feet and walked down the hall toward the bedrooms. Seconds later, she was back. "He's not in his room."

"Maybe he's helping with the livestock?"

"I hope so. That would be a good sign." She finished eating, then stood. "I'm going out to check."

"Hold on, Sylvie." He lightly grabbed her hand, preventing her from leaving. "You're not going anywhere alone."

"It's my ranch," she protested.

"I'm well aware," he drawled. He tugged on her hand. "Sit. Give me just a few more minutes to finish up. Then we'll head outside."

She didn't look happy but dropped into the chair anyway.

"Do you have any female ranch hands?" He glanced at her expectantly.

"We used to but not anymore. Why?"

"No reason." He tried not to look her in the eye, lest she guess what he was thinking. Sylvie could read him pretty well and might suspect he was looking for someone to act as her double. He downed the last of his toast and coffee, then stood. "I'm ready. Let's go."

They headed to the barn. Connor McLane was there,

grooming Storm. Sylvie smiled broadly and quickly crossed over. "I know Storm has missed you, Dad."

"Yeah, I missed him too." Connor turned to look at them. "Now what happened to the chopper?"

"It's my fault. I landed her too hard." Dawson stepped forward, ready and willing to take the blame. "I'll pay for the repairs."

"No need." Sylvie frowned at him. "It's my fault, not yours."

Connor arched a brow, his gaze bouncing between the two of them. "Why do I get the sense there's more to the story than either of you are telling me?"

Dawson hesitated, waiting for Sylvie to spill the truth, but she didn't. "Hey, thanks for helping with the horses, Dad."

"Hrmph." Her father turned back to his job of grooming Storm. "I'm sick of sitting around watching TV. Figured this was the least I could do."

Sylvie impulsively hugged her dad. "I'm so glad. There's plenty of work here for you to help with."

"Yeah, cleaning stalls is top-notch work," Connor said dryly.

"Remember what you told me and Sean when we were young? No job on a ranch is beneath a McLane."

A grin tugged at the corner of the older man's mouth. "Yeah, I remember. You used to give me the same grief I'm giving you."

"Exactly." She hugged him again. "I'll be back to help, just need to change my clothes and clean up a bit."

"No point since you're only going to smell like horse," Connor protested.

"I know. Just give me a few minutes, okay?" Sylvie left

the barn, gesturing for Dawson to follow. He and Kilo fell into step beside her.

"Maybe it's time to let him in on what's been going on," he suggested. "I know you haven't wanted to worry him because he's dealing with his cancer treatments, but he should know the danger you're facing every time you leave the house."

"Not yet." Sylvie glanced at him and grimaced. "It's only a matter of time, right? Once Sean is caught, he'll have to know."

"I like how you're thinking positive about Sean getting caught," he said. "But minimizing the danger doesn't make it go away."

"I'm aware of the danger," she snapped. Then sighed, and added, "Sorry, I'm just so frustrated by all of this."

He completely understood where she was coming from. Sylvie was one of the strongest women he'd ever met, yet everyone had a limit to what they could tolerate. "Dallas will be here later this afternoon. We'll find your brother."

"You have a plan?"

"Not yet, but hopefully soon." He paused, letting Kilo do his business. "Let's meet back in the kitchen after we clean up."

"Yeah, sure." She sounded less than enthusiastic.

He took Kilo to the guest room with him and made use of the facilities. He felt better after a shower and shave. After donning clean clothes, he headed into the kitchen. Somehow, he beat Sylvie there, so he drank another cup of coffee while he waited. Kilo stretched out at his feet, content to relax.

There had been a female deputy in town yesterday, roughly the same age and the same dark hair as Sylvie.

Maybe he could convince Deputy Holmes to ask her to help him set a trap for Sean.

If Sean knew anything about the murder of Matt Keagan, then the setup would be worth the deputy's time and energy. In fact, finding Sean may just be the key to busting up the entire gambling ring and solving the murder.

Warming to the idea, he glanced outside. Maybe a second call to Deputy Holmes would get the guy to respond faster. He made the call but was sent to the deputy's voice mail. Hearing Sylvie coming down the hall, he shortened his message to simply stating he had a plan and for Holmes to call him back. Then he pocketed his phone and took a sip of his coffee.

"Is there any more coffee left?" Sylvie asked. Kilo stood and went over to greet her. She managed a smile as she bent to rub the soft spot behind the lab's ears. To his critical eye, she still looked pale and wan, as if she was barely hanging on by a thread.

"Sure. Have this one." He handed her his cup, then turned to make another pot. "Maybe you should call Holmes again. The sooner we get the bullet removed from the chopper, the better."

She frowned. "You think the shooter will try to retrieve it?"

He shrugged. "At this point, I think anything is possible. It's what I would do if I was the shooter. Don't forget, I was trained to always expect the worst."

"Great," she muttered. "As if having to repair the bird from the original gunshot isn't bad enough, now I have to worry about more potential vandalism."

"The only easy day was yesterday." The SEAL motto came out before he could stop it.

"Gee, thanks. That's so encouraging." Sarcasm dripped from her tone.

"I'm sorry, but have faith, Sylvie. We're going to find him. As soon as Dallas arrives, we'll come up with a plan."

She didn't answer, seemingly lost in her thoughts.

He was about to reassure her again when he caught movement through the window overlooking the ranch driveway. "Hey, I think Deputy Holmes is here."

"It's about time." She finished the coffee and set the cup on the counter. He followed her outside, with Kilo beside him.

Deputy Holmes slid out from behind the wheel, eyeing them thoughtfully. "What's this about the chopper being shot down?"

Sylvie glanced at the barn, but thankfully Connor was still busy caring for the horses. "First, we were shot at while up at the mountain cave, forcing us to stay the night. Early morning, we came back down and took off in the chopper. A gunshot struck the bird, forcing Dawson to make an emergency landing."

"Sean?" Holmes asked.

"No way to say for sure," Dawson responded. "Unless you know something we don't."

"We have BOLOs out for Ned and Sean but so far without success." Holmes tipped the brim of his hat farther back on his head. "Where's the bird?"

"In the west pasture. We can take horses and ATVs to get there."

"Okay, let's go."

Dawson nodded. "Sylvie, why don't you stay here with your father? I can show Deputy Holmes where the chopper is."

"No. My chopper, my problem. We'll go together." Her chin lifted stubbornly.

"Then we need to take others with us to help keep you protected." He wasn't budging on that.

"They're busy with real work," she shot back. "I have a better idea. Kilo can hitch a ride with me, I'll drive the ATV while you and Holmes ride horses on either side of me."

He ground his teeth together, wishing for more support, but sensed that was a useless effort. He glanced at the deputy who nodded his agreement. "Fine."

"Do you have any more information on Matt Keagan's death?" Sylvie asked as Holmes traded his work shoes for cowboy boots. Then he stripped off his uniform shirt to replace it with a short-sleeved dark-green T-shirt.

"The ME has ruled his death a homicide," Holmes said grimly as they headed toward the corral.

"Drowned on purpose?" Sylvie asked in horror.

"More like clubbed on the head and left to drown," Holmes corrected. "And I need to be back in town by this afternoon, that's when they're doing the autopsy."

"Thanks for telling us," Dawson said.

Holmes sighed. "It's going to hit the news soon anyway. The witness who found the body was blabbing all over the place. Nothing is secret for long in Dillon."

Except the gambling ring, he thought with a frown.

They headed out, retracing the path they'd taken earlier that day. Dawson made sure he was positioned between Sylvie in the ATV and the mountainside since there was nowhere for the shooter to hide on the wide-open pasture.

"We didn't look for the bullet in the chopper earlier," he informed the deputy. "My priority was to keep Sylvie safe."

"Yeah, I get it," Holmes agreed. "I'm glad you both escaped without injury. There has to be a connection between Keagan's murder and these attempts against Sylvie."

"For sure," Dawson agreed. His nerves were on full alert as he continued scanning the mountainside. The chopper sat tilted to one side as the strut on the passenger side had broken when he'd landed.

The area around the bird looked vacant, but he noticed Kilo's ears perked forward. The dog could hear and smell things he couldn't, so he'd learned to trust the canine's instincts.

Dawson pulled up on the reins, bringing his gelding, Tucker, to a stop. Sylvie shut down the ATV, but Holmes went closer.

A flicker of movement from inside the chopper caught his eye. Then he noticed the window had been popped out. "No, stop!"

Holmes didn't react quick enough as a gunshot rang out. The deputy fell off his horse, the animal rearing at the sound.

Sylvie gasped, then ducked, pulling Kilo down with her.

His Sig was in his hand, and he instantly returned fire. The surprised expression on the man's face was almost comical as he slowly fell backward.

"Sean? Was that Sean?" Sylvie shot off the ATV and rushed up to peer inside.

"Not Sean," he assured her, sliding down from Tucker. "If I'm not mistaken, that's Sean's buddy, Ned Burns."

Sylvie's mouth opened, then closed again, relief flooding her features. Then she turned her attention to Deputy Holmes. The man groaned and clutched his abdomen. Dawson knew firsthand the belly was a bad place to be hit.

Ned Burns was dead, but they needed to figure out a way to get Holmes out of there before he died too.

CHAPTER FOURTEEN

Not Sean. Not Sean. Not Sean.

The phrase echoed over and over in her head as she crouched over Rick Holmes. Blood seeped from a wound off to one side of his abdomen.

"Call for a medical chopper." Dawson pulled off his shirt, scrunching it into a ball and pressing it against the wound to stop the bleeding.

She nodded, but then grimaced. "My battery is dead. I meant to charge it while we were up at the house."

"Use mine." He pulled it from his pocket, used the facial recognition to unlock it, then tossed it to her. "I have twenty percent battery left, hopefully that's enough."

She called 911, getting a different dispatcher this time rather than Brenda. "Deputy Holmes has been shot. We need a medical chopper ASAP in the west pasture of the McLane Mountain Ranch."

"Are you in danger?" the male dispatcher asked. Sylvie could hear him typing on keys in the background.

"No, Dawson Steele returned fire, the shooter is dead.

But you may want to send a deputy for that issue too. We believe the shooter was Ned Burns. He—he's in my helicopter."

"Please hold."

She stared out across the ranch, wondering how it had come to this. The assailant hiding in the chopper, shooting Deputy Holmes seconds before Dawson took him out.

Was this it then? Was the danger over? If so, where was her brother?

"We'll have a deputy respond to the scene, we request you and Dawson Steele don't touch anything at the crime scene."

"I understand." She didn't want to touch anything. Even the thought of repairing and cleaning the helicopter made her feel sick. "Please hurry on the medical chopper, though. Deputy Holmes is hurt bad."

"ETA fifteen minutes," the guy responded.

Fifteen minutes would seem like a lifetime, especially to the deputy. "Thank you." She ended the call and went over to kneel on the ground near Dawson and Deputy Holmes. Kilo was there, too, seeming to understand there was something wrong. "They're flying a crew out ASAP." She forced a smile for the deputy's sake. "Hang in there, Rick. You're going to be just fine."

"Who—did this?" There was confusion in Rick's eyes.

"Pretty sure it was Ned Burns." Dawson's gaze turned solemn. "It's my fault. I should have anticipated he'd be hiding inside the bird."

"How could you expect something like that?" Sylvie asked.

Dawson grimaced. "My job is to expect the unexpected."

Rick didn't say anything. He went limp as if he may have lost consciousness.

She felt terrible Dawson had been forced to shoot Ned Burns, but she also knew it wasn't the first time he'd had to kill someone. Yet that didn't mean he could shrug the deed off so easily. She glanced at Rick who was lying still with his eyes closed. "You saved us, Dawson." She kept her voice low. "Thank you for that."

Kilo licked Rick's hand as if to offer comfort. Dawson glanced at the lab, then turned to her. "Thank you for protecting Kilo."

"It was sheer instinct." She hadn't thought it through, and truthfully, the entire scene seemed to take place in slow motion. "I should call the house, make sure Josh knows more deputies will be arriving soon."

"Use my phone." Dawson didn't let up on the pressure he was holding against Rick's wound.

She did, grimacing when she realized it was down to 12 percent battery left. She made the call, hoping Josh would answer. Thankfully, he did. "Now what?"

She had to bite back the urge to snap at him. "Deputy Holmes has been shot, and Dawson killed the shooter. A medical chopper is on the way, but you need to escort the deputies who respond out to the west range where you picked us up earlier."

"What?" Josh sounded shocked. "Who's the shooter?"

"We believe it's Ned Burns. I'm not supposed to touch the crime scene, so I can't get close to double-check. Just— have someone escort the deputies out here and make sure my dad is safe, okay?"

"You think your dad is in danger?"

"I hope not." She wasn't sure what to think, but

Dawson's motto of expecting the unexpected made her worry. "Keep Dad with you at all times, okay?"

"Yeah, sure. I can do that." Josh sounded subdued now.

"Thanks." She disconnected from the call, hoping to preserve the last bit of battery life.

"Good idea to protect your dad," Dawson said. "He hasn't been the target yet, but that could change at any moment."

"You don't think this is over." It was a statement, not a question.

"No." Dawson looked up toward the sky as if wishing the chopper would get there soon. "We need to find your brother. Both of his friends are dead. Either he's setting this all up or he's in danger."

Neither option was good, but she nodded. "I wish I knew where to find him. I would haul him to the sheriff's department headquarters in a hot second if I could. I hate the idea of him being involved in this."

"He's involved, Sylvie. You need to resign yourself to that fact."

She knew he was right. No way could two of Sean's buddies end up dead without his being a part of whatever was going on.

The distant sound of a chopper reached them. She watched as the helicopter came in from the south, growing larger and louder as it came closer. Thankfully, there was plenty of space for the pilot to set her down, and soon two first responders wearing navy blue flight suits jumped from the bird, grabbed a gurney from the back of the chopper laden with equipment, then headed over.

Sylvie took Kilo by the collar and moved back to give them room to work. Soon Dawson joined her. The two first responders worked quickly, starting an IV, inserting a breathing tube, then packing the wound. Less than ten minutes later, they had Rick on the gurney and in the chopper. The pilot lifted off, and soon the helicopter flew out of sight.

"He's going to be make it through this," she said.

"I pray God watches over him and heals his injury. If I had only acted faster . . ." Dawson sighed heavily, then turned toward her. "What's the plan? Are we supposed to wait here for the deputies?"

"Yes. I'm sure they'll be here soon. And we're not to touch the crime scene." She rested her hand on his arm. "It's not your fault, Dawson. It's Ned Burns's fault, along with whoever else is behind this gambling ring."

He gave a terse nod but didn't say anything. She knew he still blamed himself and couldn't help feeling a similar sense of guilt.

"If we're placing blame, I need to take my fair share. I should have talked to Sean when he claimed he wanted out of ranching. I should have pressed for answers, or at least figured out something more was going on."

The sound of more ATVs approaching interrupted their conversation. The deputies made good time, maybe because one of their own was seriously injured. She slipped her hand into Dawson's, holding on tight.

He gently squeezed her fingers in response.

She pulled Dawson back a few steps. Kilo glanced around curiously, as if trying to understand all these loud noises. The posse arrived, and two deputies jumped from two ATVs driven by her ranch hands.

Josh wasn't there, and she was grateful he'd taken her concerns about sticking close to her dad to heart.

Ace led the group over. "What happened here?"

One of the deputies nudged Ace aside. "We'll take over, thanks."

Ace rolled his eyes but stepped back.

"I'm Deputy Miles, and this is Deputy Kratz," Miles said. "Tell me what happened."

Dawson told the story in a handful of succinct sentences, making Sylvie realize he'd done this before, likely reporting on his overseas missions. "The chopper was shot down earlier this morning while Sylvie and I were heading back to the ranch. I was the pilot, Sylvie was beside me, and her side was hit by gunfire. We put the bird down in a hard landing and asked for help from the ranch to get back to the house. Deputy Holmes wanted to see if he could get the bullet out of the bird, so we brought him back. A man was hiding inside and fired at us. Deputy Holmes was hit, and I returned fire, taking out the shooter."

Miles and Kratz glanced at each other. Ace and the other ranch hands looked equally shocked. Josh must not have taken the time to fill them in on the details. "Where's Deputy Holmes?"

"The medical chopper took care of him. They were planning to call the ER at Beaverhead County Hospital," Dawson informed them. "But they also talked about heading straight to the trauma center in Missoula or Helena."

She could tell that Dawson believed the trauma center was the right place for Rick Holmes.

"Okay, stay back." Deputy Miles waved his hands, indicating everyone needed to get out of the way. Miles and Kratz took several photos with their phones before approaching the helicopter. Miles whistled and looked back at Dawson. "You hit him dead center of his forehead."

"Yes." Dawson didn't elaborate.

There was a long silence before the deputies continued documenting the scene. Finally, Miles came over to Dawson. "I need your weapon."

Dawson hesitated. "Sylvie is still in danger. I need it to protect her."

Miles frowned. "I know, but you shot a man. I need your weapon to compare to the slug we find."

Dawson's expression was pained as he handed his gun to the deputy. "How quickly can I get that back?"

"I don't have an exact time frame," Miles said. "But we'll do our best."

"It's okay," she murmured in a low voice as the deputy placed Dawson's weapon in a plastic evidence bag. "There are guns at the ranch you can use."

"Handguns?"

"No, sorry. We have shotguns." She shrugged. "That's what we use against varmints around here."

"Yeah, okay. I'll make do." She could tell he wasn't happy with that answer. When they were finally released, they took one of the ATVs back to the ranch, leaving Ace and the other ranch hands to babysit the deputies.

The first thing she did when she went inside the ranch was plug in her phone. Dawson followed suit. Then her father came out and sat down. "Don't you think it's about time you tell me what's going on?"

She glanced at Dawson, who lifted a brow. He filled Kilo's water dish, then sat beside her father. The slight nod of his head encouraged her to tell her father what they knew.

And what they didn't know. Like where Sean was now.

"Okay. But a lot of this is conjecture," she warned, dropping down beside him. She took a deep breath, let it out, and started telling the sequence of events from the beginning.

————

DAWSON WATCHED the disbelief cross Connor McLane's features as Sylvie filled him in on each attack, ending the story with the recent shooting of Deputy Holmes by Ned Burns and his killing him.

"You were shot at multiple times, the barn was set on fire, and then you were almost killed while landing the chopper? How long has this been going on?" Connor demanded.

"A few days." Sylvie reached over to take her father's hand. "I didn't want to worry you, Dad. Especially with the cancer treatments you've been dealing with. But now that things have escalated—my biggest fear is that you may be in danger too."

"I'm fine," Connor protested gruffly. "You have to find Sean."

Dawson would like nothing better than to get his hands on Sean McLane. "Do you have any idea where he is? Or who he would go to if he needed a place to stay? There must be someone else, considering both his rodeo buddies are dead."

"No." Connor dragged his hands over his face. The guy looked as if he'd aged ten years in the past ten minutes. "Gambling," he muttered. "I never would have thought Sean would get involved in something like that. And now both his friends are dead . . ."

"I know." Sylvie looked at her father with sympathy. "But I think Sean is alive, Dad. I think he's hiding out from whoever is behind this."

Dawson had to admire her loyalty, misplaced though it was. He wasn't at all convinced in Sean's innocence. Maybe Sean hadn't been the one to do most of the shooting, based on Ned Burns being the one hiding in the chopper, but there was no doubt in his mind that Sean was involved in the gambling scheme all the way up to his eyeballs.

He rubbed the back of his neck, trying to think of what they were missing. He didn't know Sylvie's brother very well, but somehow, he didn't believe Sean was the mastermind of this plan.

Someone else was pulling the strings.

This Ben Stuart guy, for sure, and likely someone else. Someone local.

Considering how much time he'd spent at the McLane Mountain Ranch, he was finding it more difficult to believe one of the ranch hands were involved. Josh had proven to have an alibi for several of the incidents, so he didn't think the foreman was part of it either.

Someone in town, then. But who?

"We need to go through Sean's room," he said abruptly.

Sylvie didn't hesitate. "Let's do that now."

Connor made no move to follow them down the hall to Sean's room. Sylvie's father was obviously reeling from all the information they'd dumped in his lap.

"I'll check the dresser." Sylvie crossed over to the highboy dresser. "You check the bedside table."

He did as she asked but didn't find anything helpful. He even went so far as to slide his hands between the mattress and box spring in case Sean had hidden something there. "I've got nothing."

"Same." Sylvie turned from the dresser, scanning the room. "There must be a way to figure out where he is."

"You're sure he didn't have a girlfriend?"

She shrugged and spread her hands. "If he did, he didn't tell me. I haven't seen a picture of a girl hidden anywhere, have you?"

"No." He thought about the office. "Does he have a favorite book?"

"Sean wasn't much of a reader." She eyed him thoughtfully. "Although, now that you mention it, I do remember him grabbing a book one night about a week or two before he left. Said something about needing a boring story to put him to sleep. Interesting that it's not here, he must have returned the book to the office."

"Let's check it out." He headed for the door.

Sylvie brushed past him, leading the way into the study. She crossed to the bookcase and gazed at the book spines for a long moment. "I think he pulled something out of this section."

He peered over Sylvie's shoulder, resisting the urge to pull her into his arms. "They look like murder mysteries."

"I like murder mysteries," she said defensively. Pulling a book at random, she fanned the pages. Then another, and another.

At this rate, they'd end up going through the entire bookshelf, searching for a clue that may not even be in there.

"Dawson?" Connor called from the kitchen. "I think you have a phone call. I saw something flash across the screen."

He remembered putting the device on silent mode last night while making his way through the woods. "Coming," he called. He gestured to the bookshelf. "Let me know if you find anything."

"I will." She was still methodically removing books one at a time.

He strode down the hall into the kitchen. Connor looked pale, still shell-shocked by the news. He frowned when he saw Max Wolfe's name on the screen, indicating he had a missed call.

Picking up the device, he kept it plugged in as he returned the call. "Max? It's Dawson."

"Where have you been?" Max demanded. "I've been calling for the past twenty minutes."

"Yeah, sorry. Battery died, and I had the phone on silent." The Copper Creek Ranch foreman sounded frazzled. "What's wrong?"

"Your dad fell again, and he's refusing to go to the hospital. Oh, and he's insisting on talking to Sylvie too, no clue why. I have a lot of work to do, though, so if you could get back here to look after your dad, I'd appreciate it."

"Yeah, sure. I'm on my way." Dawson set the phone down and headed back to the office. "Find anything?"

"A phone number written on a slip of paper." Sylvie showed it to him. "Maybe it belongs to that Ben Stuart guy."

He took out his phone and called the number. The call went straight to a robotic impersonal voice mail message that instructed him to leave a message.

He didn't. He disconnected from the call. "Okay, we'll get this number to the deputies as soon as possible. In the meantime, my dad fell, and I need to get back to the Copper Creek. Max said my dad wanted to talk to you too."

"Me?" Sylvie looked surprised. "Why?"

"I don't know." Dawson thought it was strange too, but then again, maybe his dad hit his head and isn't thinking clearly. "Look, I need to get back there, and I don't want to leave you alone here while I'm gone, so you'll come with me. But you mentioned having a shotgun I can borrow?"

"Yeah, sure." She went to the rear corner of the office where a tall gun safe stood. She took a moment to unlock it, then removed a shotgun and box of Remington shells. It wasn't his Sig Sauer, but it would do in a pinch. "Here you go. Although I'm sure you have shotguns at your ranch too."

"Probably." He felt certain they did, but he didn't like being unarmed for the ride between their neighboring ranches.

Not after what had transpired in the past twenty-four hours.

Man, Dallas couldn't get to Dillon fast enough. He took a moment to check out the shotgun, appreciating that the McLane's had kept it well-oiled and clean. Then he chambered a round and carried it outside, pausing in the kitchen to grab his phone.

"Where are you going?" Connor asked.

"My dad fell again." Dawson tried not to think about what this latest fall meant for the future of the Copper Creek. "We'll be back as soon as possible."

The older man nodded. "Josh just came in to check on me. I'll head out to the barn."

"Thanks, Dad." Sylvie kissed his cheek. "Stay close to Josh. In the meantime, try to think of where we might find Sean."

"Yeah, I will." Connor sounded despondent. The news Sylvie had dumped on him was weighing him down.

Dawson led the way outside with Kilo loping along beside him. He felt bad that he hadn't given the yellow lab as much attention as he deserved. "Soon, boy," he promised as he opened the back crate area of his SUV. "We'll pick up your training program very soon."

Kilo wagged his tail and licked his face.

"Too bad more people aren't like dogs," Sylvie said wistfully.

"You've got that right." He lavished some attention on the lab, then closed the hatch. "Let's go."

He plugged his phone into the car. He'd no sooner gotten out of Sylvie's long driveway when Dallas called. "Hey, Dawg, where have you been?"

"Long story. I have to head back to the Copper Creek for a few minutes, but please tell me you're on your way."

"Just landed in Helena. You mentioned meeting me here?"

He grimaced. "Yeah, sorry, change of plan. The chopper is inoperable, so you'll need to get a car to drive to Dillon. I'm sorry about that, but it's all part of that long story I mentioned."

"Okay, no problem. Romeo and I will meet you in Dillon."

"Thanks, Dallas. See you soon."

"Later," Dallas responded before clicking off.

"Dawg?" Sylvie lifted a brow. "What is that about?"

"Team nicknames." He shrugged. "Some of the other guys got shortened versions of their names, but me? I got Dawg."

"As in you're a hot Dawg?" she teased.

"Not in the least bit." Although he had to smile. It was nice to have a bit of normalcy after the stress of the past few hours. "You should know by now, what you see is what you get."

"I do know," she said, her voice soft. "I owe you so much, Dawson."

He shifted, uncomfortable with her gratitude. He much preferred her sass. "Hey, now, don't get all soft on me. We still need to come up with a plan to find your brother."

She nodded but didn't say anything.

He took her hand and pressed a kiss along her knuckles. "We'll get through this, Sylvie. You'll see."

"Thanks." She managed a smile.

He held on to her hand throughout the entire trip to his father's ranch. When he pulled up along the driveway, one that wasn't nearly as long as Sylvie's, he noticed his father's SUV wasn't parked in the garage. Had his old man decided to go to the hospital to get medical care after all?

If so, Dawson hoped Max hadn't let him drive all by himself. Thankfully, they hadn't passed his father's vehicle along the way.

"Why do you think your dad wants to talk to me?" Sylvie asked as he shifted the vehicle into park.

"I'm hoping he's not confused from hitting his head." He pushed out of the driver's side, then went around back to free Kilo.

The front door of the house was open about an inch. He frowned and quickened his pace. Had something happened after he'd spoken to Max?

Had his father taken a turn for the worst?

"Dad? Max?" He shouted as he barreled into the house. Sylvie and Kilo were right behind him. He made it only a few steps inside when he stopped short.

"Come in, Dawg, and close the door." Max Wolfe was standing near the fireplace, holding a handgun pointed directly at his chest. "Oh good, you brought Sylvie. That's who I really wanted to see."

Dawson froze, the last piece of the puzzle falling into place. "You're the brains behind the gambling scheme. Or maybe you're just Ben Stuart's puppet."

"Who said Navy SEALs were all brawn and no brains?" Max drawled. "Put your hands on your head where I can see them. You too, Sylvie."

Dawson didn't dare glance at Sylvie. The shotgun he'd borrowed was out of reach in his SUV, and his MK 3 knife was in a holder on his belt.

He stared at his father's ranch foreman, knowing he had only one option. Sacrificing himself to save Sylvie.

CHAPTER FIFTEEN

Max Wolfe. She'd had him on her list of suspects early on but then dismissed the idea. After talking things through with Dawson, his involvement hadn't made sense. Especially since she'd assumed Max would get the Copper Creek after Dawson moved back to California.

Only now it did make sense. Max must have been a part of the gambling ring, maybe funded originally by Stuart. Only the guys got in debt. Sean must have been paying him off a little at a time until he couldn't come up with any more cash.

Because she'd cut him off.

She glared at Max, ignoring the gun in his hand. She sensed he wouldn't shoot them here inside the house. He didn't look like the kind of guy to bother cleaning up a mess.

No, he'd take them somewhere their bodies would never be found.

"Where's my brother?" she demanded.

A flicker of uncertainty crossed Max's gaze. "You tell me. Your baby brother owes me and my boss a lot of money.

That idiot promised me he'd find a way to sell the ranch to pay off his debt."

No surprise there, she and Dawson had already figured that much out for themselves. The missing piece was standing in front of them.

"You had Ned Burns working for you, is that it?" Dawson asked. "You made sure he followed Sylvie, took shots at her, started the barn fire, and instigated all those other attempts, right? Although you must have been the guy driving the black Ford truck that I took out on the road."

Max's expression hardened. "I wasn't happy about you shooting the gas tank. But Ned? Yeah, he was paying off his debt. It was Sean's idea to scare Sylvie into selling the ranch, but then he got chicken. I was the one who had to take things a little farther." Max narrowed his gaze. "You know too much, Dawg. Good thing I'd already planned to get rid of you."

Dawson moved a step closer, his hands still on his head. Sylvie could tell he was trying to put himself between her and Max. Kilo sensed something was amiss and began to growl. She found herself wondering if the dog knew how to attack on command. Dawson continued talking. "Do you know Ned Burns is dead? I killed him."

Another flicker of unease darkened Max's gaze. But it quickly disappeared. "Take one more step, Dawg, and I'll shoot. When you're out of the way, Sylvie and I can come to some sort of—agreement."

Over my dead body, Sylvie thought. Then she swallowed hard because that was a very real possibility.

"I don't know where Sean is," Sylvie said, trying to draw Max's attention from Dawson. "I've been looking for days now, checking his usual haunts, without success."

Max shrugged. "I'll deal with him later. It doesn't much

matter where he is once I get the deed to the McLane Mountain Ranch."

"Where's my dad?" Dawson asked. "What have you done to him?"

"He has a follow-up doctor's appointment today, so he'll be gone for hours." Max smirked. "Something you might have known if you'd been here recently. By the time your old man returns, it will be too late."

Sylvie winced, sensing Dawson's guilt. But he didn't move or react in any way to Max's statement.

"You know, Max, you didn't think this little plan through very well." Dawson slid the barest of an inch closer. "My dad is going to have a lot of questions about how you managed to obtain the McLane Mountain Ranch. And since your buddy Ned shot Deputy Holmes, the entire police force in Dillon will do everything in their power to get to the bottom of the attempted murder of a fellow cop. It won't take them long to figure out you're the link to Ben Stuart and the illegal gambling ring. They already suspect Stuart, by the way." Dawson shook his head, making a *tsk-tsk* sound. "You'll never get away with this."

"Oh, Sylvie here is going to make sure I do. Won't you, darlin'?" The way Max leered at her caused nausea to churn in her belly. "I admit, this wasn't the original plan, but I can adapt. Sylvie is a looker; I won't mind having her as my wife."

It was all she could do not to vomit. "I wouldn't marry you if you were the last man on the planet."

"Oh, I think you will." Max flashed an evil smile. "You wouldn't want any harm to come to your daddy now, would you?"

The implication was clear. Sylvie stared at him in horror. There had to be a way to get out of this mess.

"Blah, blah, blah," Dawson drawled. "The sheriff's department will figure it all out, and the marriage will either never happen or be annulled. Honestly, Max, I expected better from you. I give you credit for working with Stuart on the gambling scheme, but since then, you've failed in so many ways." There was emphasis on the word failed.

"Shut up!" Max shouted, his face reddening with anger. "I'll kill you here and make Sylvie clean up the mess."

Kilo growled louder now, baring his teeth in a way Sylvie had never seen the lab do. Kilo had always been sweet and happy, but not now.

"Get that dog out of here," Max said. He moved the gun enough to point the barrel at her, then moved it back to Dawson. "Now!"

She swallowed hard, trying to think of what to do. Leaving Dawson wasn't an option. But she wasn't armed either. She wanted to protect Kilo, too, but knew getting the dog away from his owner wouldn't be easy.

The muscles in Dawson's body tensed, and she instantly knew he was planning to launch himself at Max in a last-ditch effort to protect her. The only possible weapon nearby was a ceramic lamp on the table, but it was more than an arm's length away.

"Now!" Max repeated, his voice louder than ever.

"Attack!" she shouted the command at the top of her lungs as she lunged for the lamp. The lab rushed forward, clamping his jaw around Max's ankle at the exact same time Dawson surged forward, his long fingers grabbing at the gun in Max's hand.

A gunshot rang out as the two men struggled. She picked up the lamp and moved around Kilo who was hanging on tightly to Max's leg. Then she brought the lamp down on Max's head with as much strength as she could muster.

Max slumped to the floor beneath the blow. Dawson wrenched the gun from his hand, then glanced down at Kilo who still had his jaw locked around Max's ankle. "It's okay, boy. Let go." He gently removed the dog. Then he glanced at her. "Nice work, Sylvie. Although I was hoping you would have gotten out of here."

"You wouldn't have left me either, and you know it." She raked her gaze over him, frowning when she saw blood staining his T-shirt. "You're hit?"

Dawson stepped back, looking down at the unconscious Max Wolfe. Then he put a hand to his side. "Bullet grazed my side, nothing too serious."

"Are you sure?" She moved closer, raking the hem of his T-shirt up so she could examine the wound. There was a bloody furrow along his left side, which was bleeding but didn't look too deep. The series of scars crisscrossing his abdomen, though, gave her pause. He'd mentioned several surgeries, but the angry-looking raised ridges marring his skin stole her breath. "Oh, Dawson," she murmured.

"Hey, I told you it was just a graze." He gently pushed her hand aside. "Find me some rope so we can tie him up. I'll call the sheriff's department. At least this time the perp isn't dead. Hopefully, Max will tell what he knows about Ben Stuart."

She forced herself to nod. "I'm sure there's some in the tack room." She made the trip outside, startled to see the sun shining brightly overhead. It seemed wrong after being held at gunpoint.

The barn was empty, the stalls were too. She wondered where Max had sent all the ranch hands, then decided it didn't matter. Better really that they weren't in danger.

She found the rope. As she headed back out to the house, a man stepped out from the shadows holding a shotgun.

Sean.

She froze, unsure whether she could trust her own flesh and blood. The shotgun could have been the one Dawson had left in the SUV, or it could have been one that Sean had taken two weeks ago.

"Where's Max?" Sean asked, his gaze shifting back and forth nervously. He looked terrible, his face and clothes were dirty and torn, his chin covered with a shaggy beard.

"I hit him on the head with a lamp while Dawson wrestled the gun from him. We'll use this"—she lifted the rope—"to tie him up." Then a flash of anger hit hard. "Where have you been? Do you have any idea what I've been through these past few days? I'm lucky to be alive, Sean, no thanks to you."

"I know, I'm sorry. I've been hiding in the mountains, trying to find a way to get to Max." He pointed the barrel of the shotgun down at the ground. "I saw Landon leave in his SUV and thought maybe I could confront Max once and for all. But then you and Dawson showed up, and I figured I'd better wait."

"Wait? For what? For us to be killed?" She was irrationally irritated with her brother. "Max held a gun on us, did you know that? He was planning to shoot Dawson and force me to marry him!"

"Look, Sylvie, I'm sorry . . ."

"Stop!" She held up her hand, unwilling to listen to more excuses. "Just stop. We'll talk more later. For now, we need your help."

"Uh, sure." The way Sean glanced around nervously gave her pause. "I can help tie up Max."

"Come with me." She continued walking up to the house, watching her brother from the corner of her eye. She still didn't trust him. Slowing her pace, she moved the rope to her left hand, waited until Sean was next to her, then made a grab for the shotgun. Catching him by surprise worked. Ripping the shotgun away, she took a step back, brought the weapon up to her shoulder, and pointed it at him.

"W-what are you doing?" Sean stuttered.

"You think I'm buying this act of yours? Think again." She stared at him without flinching. "Don't make me shoot you."

"Sylvie?" Dawson came to the doorway. The corner of his mouth quirked up in a smile as he roughly grabbed Sean's shoulders. "Well, lookie here. Nice job, Sylvie. We've got both of them now."

"I swear I was coming to help," Sean insisted, stumbling as Dawson wrenched both of his arms behind his back.

"Maybe, maybe not," Sylvie said bluntly. "Either way, we'll let the sheriff's department figure it out." Sylvie dropped the bundled rope to the floor and kicked it toward Dawson, still holding the shotgun ready. He picked it up and used his wicked knife to cut off a length to use on Sean's wrists. Then he went back into the living room to tie up Max Wolfe. The ranch foreman was groaning and moving around, which was a good sign. She was secretly glad Dawson hadn't been forced to kill him. The poor guy had enough of that while serving his country.

Soon both men were securely tied up. Sylvie finally lowered the shotgun.

It was over.

DAWSON TOOK the shotgun from Sylvie's hands, checking it closely. It was dirty and dusty, which made him think it wasn't the one he'd left in the SUV. He set it aside, then looked at Sean. "A couple of deputies will be here shortly. As it turns out, they were at Sylvie's ranch, so it won't take them long to make their way here."

Sean darted furtive looks around the room. "Yeah, okay. I understand."

"No, I don't think you do." Sylvie stepped forward and stabbed her finger into her brother's chest. "You're going to be honest about everything, Sean. Do you hear me? You're going to come clean about the gambling, about what you know about Ben Stuart and Max Wolfe, the money you stole from the ranch, and about how your good buddy Matt Keagan ended up dead in the Beaverhead River."

"Matt's dead?" Sean paled and staggered backward a few steps in a way that didn't seem fake. "What are you talking about? When? How?"

"He was murdered." Anger sparked Sylvie's green eyes.

"I—didn't know." Sean sank onto a chair and dropped his chin to his chest. "I swear I didn't know," he whispered again.

Dawson eyed Sylvie, who didn't look the least bit sympathetic. And really, he couldn't blame her. Maybe Sean wasn't as guilty as they'd originally thought, but he certainly hadn't helped the situation by disappearing.

"How much money did he owe Max?" Sylvie demanded.

"I—a lot. We all did." Sean raised dull eyes to meet his sister's gaze. "I kept thinking we'd start winning and be able to pay Max back, but that didn't happen."

That was always the gambler's mindset. One more hand, one more game, and their luck would change.

He moved over to where Max was lying on his side. "How exactly did you win all that money, Max? Did you cheat? Huh? Use a marked deck?"

Sean gaped and stared at the foreman in shock. "Did you?"

Max clenched his jaw shut, refusing to say a word. But that alone made Dawson suspect the guy had, in fact, cheated. Maybe on Stuart's orders. Or just to get a bigger cut of the cash.

Most gambling was a game of chance. And that usually meant that winning and losing went back and forth. Some of the guys deployed overseas would play cards, but that hadn't interested him. But he had noticed that one guy would win big one day, then lose the next.

He nodded to himself. "The cops will figure out if you used a marked deck, Max. Although the whole gambling scheme isn't your biggest problem. No, being arrested for murder is. That will get you life behind bars without any possibility of parole."

"I didn't kill anyone," Max blurted. "That was all Ned Burns."

Dawson shrugged. "That's for the cops to figure out. And since Burns is dead, and you're still here . . ." He spread his hands wide. "I think they'll try to pin it all on you. Besides, conspiracy to commit murder carries the same sentence. Unless you decide to talk about Stuart's involvement to save yourself some prison time."

Max stared at him in hatred but remained silent. A squad pulled up near the house, and the same two deputies who'd been down at the chopper murder scene emerged from the vehicle, hands resting on their weapons.

Dawson sighed, bending down to rub Kilo's ears before going out to meet them. This would be another long day. Yet knowing the danger to Sylvie was finally over helped.

"Did you kill another guy?" Deputy Miles demanded.

"No, sir. Sylvie hit him on the head with a lamp"—he gestured to the broken ceramic scattered across the floor—"while I disarmed him."

"Hrmph." The two deputies looked around the room, taking in the two men who were tied up. "Okay, start at the beginning," Miles said wearily.

He and Sylvie spent the next hour explaining what happened. Sean remained silent at first, but then admitted to his role in gambling to the point he owed Max a hundred thousand dollars.

Sylvie's jaw dropped, but Dawson had figured as much. Still, Sylvie's ranch was worth millions, so Max was being a greedy son of a gun to expect the entire property in exchange for that debt.

Sean also admitted to firing the first shot toward Sylvie while she was at the north ridge. When she'd almost died, he'd backed out of the deal, leaving Matt and Ned to deal with Max. As he'd hidden in the mountains, he'd thought about going after Max himself and had started watching the Copper Creek for Max's movements.

The deputies finally left, taking both Max and Sean with them. Max kept insisting he needed medical care, but the deputies simply promised he'd be seen once they were back in Dillon.

"I'm worried about your father," Sylvie said. "He can't run the ranch alone. Do you have any idea who amongst your ranch hands can step into the foreman role?"

"No clue," he admitted. "But we'll figure out something."

"We?" Sylvie frowned. "You're not staying."

True, sticking around had not been a part of his plan. But he stepped toward Sylvie, lifting a hand to her hair. "I'm not going anywhere."

"Dawson . . ." She sighed, then threw herself into his arms. "I was never so scared in my life when I realized you were going to throw yourself at Max."

"How did you know?" He cradled her close.

"Because I know you, and I saw you go tense." She lifted her head to meet his gaze. "That's why I told Kilo to attack. I wasn't sure the lab would do that, but I was hoping to distract Max long enough to hit him with the lamp."

"Ah, perfect timing," he murmured. Then he lowered his head to kiss her. It seemed like forever since he'd held her in his arms, since he'd savored her taste. And somewhere in the dim recesses of his mind, he knew his heart would always be here in Dillon, Montana.

With her.

And for the first time since returning home, he didn't feel the least bit suffocated. Instead, his heart swelled with hope and love.

They could always take vacations, right? Visit places he'd always wanted to see. Showing Sylvie parts of the world. They could do whatever they wanted as long as they returned home.

"Well, now, seems like our Dawg has gotten himself a pretty little filly."

Dallas's voice intruded on his thoughts, forcing him to reluctantly break off from Sylvie's kiss. He barely glanced at his swim buddy, Dallas, and Romeo, his chocolate lab. "Go away, Dallas. I don't need you anymore."

"Dawson, don't be rude." Sylvie turned to smile at the newcomer. "It's nice to meet you, Dallas. I'm Sylvie McLane."

Dallas smiled broadly, clearly enjoying this far too much. "Nice to meet you, too, Sylvie. I'm Dallas Hoffman, and this is my sidekick, Romeo." The two dogs, Kilo and Romeo, sniffed each other's butts, then began to play. "And what do you mean you don't need me anymore? I came all this way to cover your six!"

Dawson sighed, slipping his arm around Sylvie's waist to keep her close. "I really appreciate that, Dallas, but turns out that Sylvie was able to knock our bad guy out with a lamp and disarm another suspect, so the danger is finally over."

"Ya gotta love a resourceful woman." Dallas sent Sylvie a wink. He had tanned skin and blond hair, longer than how he'd worn it through their Navy SEAL days. The guy was pure Texan and proud of it.

Dawson scowled. "Hands off, she's mine."

"Excuse me?" Sylvie turned to look at him. "I'm not a dog like Kilo. Or Romeo," she added, eyeing the two dogs playing at their feet. "I don't belong to anyone."

"Except God," Dawson said. "And I didn't mean to insinuate anything bad, it's just that Dallas flirts with everyone, it's his worst personality trait." Dawson's expression turned serious. "Sylvie, I know this might come as a surprise, but I've fallen in love with you."

"Love?" She gaped, then frowned. "Dawson, you've been telling me since the first time we reconnected that you're not sticking around, now you suddenly want to stay in Montana and you love me? That's a lot to swallow. I'm sure that in less than a week you'll be itching to leave."

"It's true I didn't want to stick around or fall in love. But God apparently had other plans for me." He smiled and pulled her close. "Trust me, Sylvie, I have fallen head over heels in love with you. And if you need time, that's fine. I'll prove I'm here to stay."

"Dawg doesn't make promises he can't keep," Dallas spoke up. "He's saved my life more times than I can count."

"Thanks, Dallas, but I've got this." He scowled at his swim buddy.

"I'm not sure you do." Dallas crossed his arms over his chest, looking skeptical. "The pretty lady doesn't trust you. I'm just trying to let her know she can."

"Honestly, you two, knock it off." Sylvie shook her head. "I trusted Dawson to keep me safe these past few days. It's not that. I just know that he, well, both of you have traveled the world." Her gaze flickered with uncertainty. "I've barely left Montana, and that was only to buy horses or other livestock."

"Ah, Sylvie." Dawson cupped her cheek with his hand. "There are many places I'd like to take you to visit, beautiful places with stunning views, but please believe me, McLane Mountain and Copper Creek will always be home."

She still didn't look convinced. Dawson knew he'd have to show her how much she meant to him over time.

"It's okay. There's no rush." He drew her in for another hug and a quick kiss. "I can be patient."

"I can't," Dallas complained. "I want to see how this ends."

Dawson rolled his eyes. "Go away, Dallas."

"After he's come all this way?" Sylvie shook her head. "It's not like you can't use the help around here, Dawson, especially since your ranch foreman was just taken away in handcuffs."

"Happy to help, Dawg," Dallas said, grinning like a fiend.

"Fine. Grab your stuff, I'll show you to the guest room."

It hit him hard that he wouldn't be staying close to Sylvie any longer. He didn't want to leave her side, regardless of the fact that she wasn't in danger anymore.

Dallas finally left them alone. He looked into Sylvie's eyes. "I hope you'll give me a chance, Sylvie. I love you so much."

Her expression softened, and she surprised him by drawing him down for another kiss. A nice, long, leisurely kiss. He would have preferred to stand there holding Sylvie close forever, but his idiot teammate interrupted them again.

"Never mind, I'll find the guest room," Dallas said loudly.

"Shut up and go away," Dawson muttered.

Sylvie chuckled. "You two crack me up."

He would have rather had Sylvie all to himself, but obviously Dallas wasn't going to help, despite his claim to do just that. "When can I see you again? I liked staying with you. I don't want to lose what we had."

"Aw, you won't." She kissed him again. "I love you too, Dawson. Since the first moment we kissed in my kitchen. But I don't want to hold you back in any way."

"Hold me back?" He grinned like a loon, picked her up, and swung her around. He gave her a quick kiss, then gazed into her eyes. "You've made me the happiest man in the world, Sylvie. I promise we'll make this work."

"And Dawg always keeps his promises," Dallas drawled.

Dawson closed his eyes for a moment, envisioning his buddy disappearing in a puff of smoke. But, of course, that wasn't going to happen.

"You know how to ride, don't you, Dallas?" Dawson asked.

"Does a pig know how to eat?" Dallas shot back.

"Make yourself useful and head out to the barn." He continued looking down at Sylvie. "You can pick a horse to ride, I'll join you soon."

"Soon?" Dallas snorted. "Sure thing."

"I hate letting you go, but I should probably drive you home," he murmured. "I'll have to come back here, though, because of Dallas and also because of my dad. When he returns home from his doctor's appointment, I'll have to break the news about Max." Dawson never minded hard work, whether it was working the ranch or getting through a tough SEAL op.

But he found himself resentful of the time he'd be forced to spend away from Sylvie.

"I wouldn't mind taking a horseback ride," Sylvie said. "You've seen most of my ranch, but I haven't seen much of the Copper Creek." She entwined her arms around his neck and pulled him down into another kiss. "And maybe we can work out an arrangement where we jointly work these two ranches for a bit."

"I love you so much," Dawson whispered. He kissed her with all his heart and soul, then reluctantly pulled away. "Just promise me you won't fall for Dallas. I wasn't kidding about him being a chick magnet."

"Aw, Dawson." She took his hand as they walked outside. "My heart already belongs to you."

Her love was a gift he didn't deserve but one he'd cherish for the rest of his life.

EPILOGUE

Three weeks later . . .

Sylvie sat on Fanny's back in the same spot on the north ridge as she had almost a month ago. Dawson was on Storm beside her. Dallas had stayed for a full week before heading back home, muttering something about his sister needing help again. Landon, Dawson's dad, had been shocked to learn of Max's attempts to kill them and was grateful for Dawson's support in running the ranch now that Max was in jail.

"Sean may get off with a lighter sentence," she told Dawson. "His lawyer is trying to get his prison time whittled down from ten years to five." She glanced at the man she loved. "I'm not sure I want him back on the ranch, though. Not unless he promises to get help."

"Five years in jail will be plenty of time for him to see the light." Dawson shrugged. "If he does want to return, make him work without granting him access to the money. He can get paid every week just like the rest of the guys. Frankly, I'm still angry with him for what he put you through."

"I know, I'm not happy with that either." Deputy Miles had let them know that Deputy Holmes was doing okay and that they'd found a bit of leather from a belt near the spot where Matt Keagan's body had been found. The missing bit was a perfect match to the belt that Max Wolfe was wearing when he'd been arrested. It was enough for them to file a first degree murder charge against Max Wolfe for Keagan's death. That in turn had caused Max to open up about working for Ben Stuart, who was the mastermind behind the gambling ring. Apparently, there were several others taking place in other mountain towns, with Stuart giving each of the local site managers, in this case, Max, a cut of the profits.

Hard to imagine that this was going on in small-town Dillon.

Rick and Marty had gone to the Feds since Ben Stuart had property in several states. They caught up to him in Colorado, no connection to her ex-husband, and he was cooling his heels in a federal prison. A follow-up on her ex-husband, Paul Griffin, proved he was still in Colorado and once again engaged to be married. The woman sold real estate and apparently had a beautiful home in the mountains.

She was relieved Sean hadn't been directly responsible for killing his buddy Matt. Or for doing anything other than the first attempt against her.

Which was bad enough.

"Hey, I'll support anything you decide, Sylvie." Dawson smiled. "We're in this together, remember?"

"We are." She couldn't deny that Dawson seemed content with living and working the ranch. She'd half expected him to take off by now, but he'd more than pulled his weight. Their ranch hand, Ace, had asked to be considered for the Copper Creek foreman position, and Dawson had agreed to give him a try.

So far, Ace was more than proving himself worthy of the position. Josh and Ace talked often about sharing ranch hands to help keep costs down.

Dawson swung out of his saddle, then tied Storm to a tree. He offered her a hand, but she'd been getting off horses since she was eight and managed just fine. There were times Dawson tried to do the heavy lifting, and she had to constantly remind him she was more than capable of doing the work.

But it was sweet that he cared.

"It's so beautiful here, Sylvie." Dawson drew her to a spot that offered a panoramic view of the ranch. The spot where he'd rescued her from the cliff. "I figured this was the right place to do this."

"To do what?" She glanced at him curiously. "Did you pack a picnic?"

"You must have smelled the fried chicken," he teased. Then he shocked her by dropping to one knee. Then he offered her a simple band with small diamonds, one that wouldn't get in the way of doing ranch chores. "Sylvie McLane, will you please marry me?"

"Yes, Dawson. I'll marry you." She held out her left hand so he could slide the ring on. "You know me so well, don't you?"

"I'm learning more every hour we spend together," he admitted. He rose and pulled her into his arms. "I love you so much. I have one request. Will you let me take you someplace fun for our honeymoon?"

She laughed. "Sure, as long as it's a place you haven't been either. That way we can explore it together."

"Done. I'm thinking we'll go to Fiji. I've never been there, and I think you'd look amazing in a grass skirt."

She shook her head. "I'll go to Fiji, but no guarantees on the grass skirt."

He pretended to look disappointed, then his gaze turned serious. "I love you, Sylvie. We'll figure out a way to make this work with our respective ranches. I would never ask you to leave your home."

She kissed him, and it took several minutes for his words to register. "What do you mean, make our respective ranches work?"

He arched a brow. "I'm not taking your ranch, Sylvie. It's yours and yours alone."

"Oh, Dawson." She smiled and shook her head. "Of course, we'll combine our ranches. It would be silly not to. And I'm sure that will make our fathers very happy."

Instead of smiling and nodding in agreement, he frowned. "I'm not taking any part of your ranch, Sylvie. End of story."

The fact that he was arguing over this only made her love him more. "Please, Dawson. I really want us to combine our properties." She rested her hand against his cheek and added, "Think of our children."

"Children?" He looked momentarily panicked, then grinned. "Okay, it's a deal. We'll join the properties for the sake of our kids." He kissed her, then added, "We'd better get married sooner rather than later. I'm not getting any younger."

"Okay, how's next month sound?"

"Maybe next week?" Dawson grinned. "Whatever you want is fine with me."

Next week worked too. She didn't want or need a big splashy wedding.

She just needed him. Now and forever.

I HOPE you enjoyed Sylvie and Dawson's story in *Sealed with Strength*. Are you ready to read Dallas and Maggie's story in *Sealed with Trust?* Click here!

DEAR READER

I hope you are enjoying my Called to Protect series. I'm having fun writing about these Navy SEAL heroes who are struggling with the pain of losing a teammate while trying to adapt to civilian life. The least I could do was help them find love. I hope you enjoyed Sylvie and Dawson's story. I love the mountains and really had fun placing their story on a ranch in Montana.

I'm hard at work finishing up Dallas and Maggie's story in *Sealed with Trust*. My goal is to have all six books finished before the end of the year, although I do have several books under contract with Harlequin too. Trust me, I'm writing as fast as I can!

I adore hearing from my readers! I can be found through my website at https://www.laurascottbooks.com, via Facebook at https://www.facebook.com/ LauraScottBooks, Instagram at https://www.instagram. com/laurascottbooks/, and Twitter https://twitter.com/ laurascottbooks. Also, take a moment to sign up for my monthly newsletter, all subscribers receive a free novella,

Starting Over, that is not available for purchase on any platform.

Until next time,

Laura Scott

PS: If you're interested in a sneak peek of *Sealed with Trust*, I've included the first chapter here.

SEALED WITH TRUST

Chapter one

"What time are you coming home?" Laney asked.

"Soon, sweetie." Maggie Chandler smiled as she spoke to her eight-year-old daughter using the hands-free function in her police-issued SUV. "Tell Nanna I'll be home for dinner, okay?"

"We're having spaghetti and meatballs!" Laney's voice rose with excitement. "My favorite."

"Yum," Maggie agreed, shaking her head wryly. Her mother would do anything to make Laney happy. Maggie was blessed to have her mother's help in watching her daughter while she was at work. "See you soon."

"Okay, bye." Laney disconnected from the call.

Maggie's smile faded when she noticed several buzzards dropping from the sky to land on a particular area in the dry, hot, central Texas landscape. Likely a dead animal, but her cop instincts jangled enough that she slowed her speed and took the SUV off-road toward the flock of birds. At nearly four o'clock in the afternoon, the sun was still high enough to make it difficult to see, even with her sunglasses. As she grew closer, she saw a lumpy shape lying on the ground. It was bigger than a coyote but smaller than a cow. Too wide to be a deer. Not long enough to be a horse.

The birds flew back up into the sky as she approached, but they continued to circle up above, waiting patiently for her to leave so they could get back to their feast.

Two minutes later, she swallowed hard when she recognized the lumpy shape wasn't an animal, but human. Based on the buzzards, she felt certain the person was dead, but she knew she needed to be sure. Quickly hitting the brake, she threw the vehicle into park and killed the engine. When she stepped out into the stifling August heat, the acrid scent told her everything she needed to know.

The person was dead and had been for at least a few hours. Probably longer.

The August heat was oppressive as usual, and she instantly began to sweat despite her short-sleeved blue blouse and thin dress slacks. As one of three detectives for the criminal investigative unit of the Fredericksburg police department, this wasn't her first dead body. But crime in this small, quaint tourist town was generally related to sexual assaults, drugs, or alcohol abuse.

Not murder.

Granted, she knew better than to assume foul play. It was possible this victim had gotten drunk and died out here of natural causes, but that scenario wasn't likely. For one thing, she was in the middle of highway 16, not anywhere near any bars or taverns. There also wasn't a vehicle nearby. How had the victim gotten here? Walked? Or had been dropped off by a friend or rideshare? She swept her gaze over the area, her investigative mind spinning with various possibilities.

Moving cautiously as to not disturb the crime scene, she edged closer. The hard dry ground didn't reveal footprints that she could see.

It only took a moment to identify the body as male, lying partially on his side. She angled around toward the feet to get a better look. Then abruptly reared back when she recognized the victim as Tate Chandler, her ex-husband. His face had already been pecked at by the birds, but there was no mistaking his bright red hair, his beard, and his bicep tattoo where he'd inked her name. *Maggie.*

There was also a bullet hole in the center of his forehead.

Covering her hand with her mouth, she turned and hurried back to the SUV. She needed to call this in. She fumbled with her phone, feeling like a rookie patrol officer on her first day.

"Dispatch, this is Detective Chandler. I'm ten miles outside of town on highway 16 and found a body. Victim appears to be former Fredericksburg police officer Tate Chandler."

"Your husband?" Dispatcher Delilah Hall asked, her voice high and squeaky.

"Ex-husband." She leaned weakly against her SUV, wishing she could erase the image of Tate's dead face from her mind. "And you need to let Lieutenant Fernando know because there's a bullet hole in the center of his forehead and no gun lying nearby to be self-inflicted. I have no doubt this is a homicide."

Delilah audibly gasped. "You can't work the case, Maggie, that's a conflict of interest. I'll call Simmons."

She knew that was true, the vic being her ex was absolutely a conflict of interest. Yet their police department was very small, so she doubted she'd be able to avoid participating in the investigation. Maybe they'd give her the menial tasks to do. "Let Fernando know I'll be here waiting for the rest of the team."

"Will do."

Maggie pocketed her phone, feeling sick at seeing her ex-husband's dead body. She and Tate had been divorced for four years now, and he'd recently started causing trouble again over their custody arrangement. After being mostly nonexistent in Laney's life the past four years, suddenly he wanted to pick up where he'd left off before their divorce. As if Laney was still the four-year-old who'd fawned over him, rather than the cheeky eight-year-old who barely asked about her father. Deep down, it irritated her because Tate knew the truth and was simply using Laney as a pawn in his war against her. But knowing that didn't change the situation, so she'd been forced to call her lawyer to deal with his latest threat. Tate's plan was to have Laney stay with him in Austin during the entire school year where the academics were allegedly so much better than what Fredericksburg had to offer. Oh, and his schedule was so much better than hers, too, with less call hours. She'd tried to point out that Laney had friends here and that she barely knew her father anymore, but Tate had insisted he was only doing what was best for their daughter.

Yeah, right. After barely seeing her except at Christmas and two weeks during the summer, even that being two years ago? Not.

Their last conversation played over in her mind. Like she was the bad mother who didn't care about Laney's education and well-being instead of the other way around.

Now he was dead. Murdered. Who would so such a thing? And why?

She turned back to look at the scene, again wondering why his body had been left all the way out here in the middle of nowhere. A couple of brave buzzards had dropped back down to the body.

"Hiya! Go away!" She waved her arms and jumped up and down to shoo them off. A little like closing the barn door after the horses escaped, but she couldn't stand the idea of them going after Tate's dead body.

She didn't love him, which had been the real reason their marriage hadn't lasted. But she had cared about him. At least in the beginning.

Her mind was still reeling when Lieutenant Antonio Fernando arrived, followed shortly thereafter by Kent Simmons. Both men looked grim as they approached.

"Maggie." Fernando greeted her with a nod. "What happened?"

"I was making my last round through the area. I happened to notice the buzzards circling overhead and came over to investigate." She gestured toward the scene to their right. "I only went close enough to recognize the dead victim as Tate and that he'd been murdered. I didn't touch anything at the crime scene."

The lieutenant exchanged a concerned glance with Kent Simmons. "Okay, stay here. We'll check it out."

Hanging back wasn't easy. Despite being the youngest detective on their small team and a woman, she was usually treated fairly. Simmons, who was ten years her senior, often worked cases with her, under Fernando's tutelage.

But not this time, she realized grimly. No, this time, she'd be kept out of the information loop. At least initially, while Simmons retraced Tate's last movements.

She thought about their angry conversation just last night. About how she'd accused him of retaliating against her for the divorce by attacking their joint custody agreement. After all, he was the one who'd quit the Fredericksburg police force. He was the one who'd relocated ninety miles away to Austin for his new job working private security for some rich guy. He was the one who'd always had a reason he couldn't come visit or have her drop Laney to Austin per the co-custody agreement. Now he was sending her legal paperwork to challenge their agreement? She'd pretty much told him that would only happen over her dead body.

Now he was dead.

A chill snaked over her, despite the hot sun. She abruptly frowned. Had Tate been in Austin last night when he'd called? Or had he been here in Fredericksburg? That he was here now, made her think the latter. Her first thought was to get his phone records, to track his calls and where he'd been, then remembered it wasn't her case.

Blowing out a long breath, she watched as the Lieutenant and Simmons walked around the body, taking photos with their phones and speaking in hushed tones. Turning toward the highway, she could see the boxy shape of the forensic van heading toward the scene. It would take a while to search for evidence, especially since small animals could have carried some away. Would they let her help search? Or send her straight home?

Belatedly, she winced, thinking of the conversation she'd need to have with Laney. The little girl had lost the only father figure she'd ever known. Telling Laney she'd never see her father again would be heartbreaking.

The only bright side was that Laney rarely asked about

her dad. His being in Austin had created a rift between them. No bad feelings, just more of an out of sight, out of mind scenario.

Maybe it was her fault, Maggie thought wearily. Maybe she should have tried harder to make things work. She could have considered moving to Austin, most police departments were hiring these days. But she hadn't wanted to give up her position here in Fredericksburg. Simmons had spoken of retiring in a few years, had even put money down on a nice property near the ocean in Corpus Christi. His leaving would make her the senior detective.

Had her selfishness contributed to Tate's death?

As soon as the thought entered her mind, she shook it off. Her not moving to Austin hadn't put the bullet hole in Tate's forehead. A person had done that. But who? And why?

"Maggie?" Lieutenant Fernando's voice interrupted her thoughts.

"Yes?" She turned to face him. Her boss was striding toward her with an enigmatic expression on his face. "Did you find something?"

He hesitated. "No, but I'd like to ask you a few questions."

"Sure, although I'm not sure how much I can help."

"When did you last see or hear from your ex-husband?"

"I haven't seen him in well over two years, but I spoke to him last night. He got some crazy idea to challenge the custody agreement despite not seeing Laney as often as he was scheduled to in the first place."

"You argued?" Fernando asked.

Her instincts went on high alert, and she wished she'd chosen her words more carefully. Having an argument with a man who'd recently been murdered made her look like a suspect. "We had a conversation," she said, backpedaling. "I told him our lawyers would need to talk if he wanted to change the agreement."

"That means fighting it out in court, right?" Fernando asked.

Her cheeks flushed and beads of sweat rolled down from her temples, not just because of the one-hundred-degree temps. She didn't like sitting on the hot seat like some perp. "To be honest, I didn't think he was serious about the proposal. Like I said, he rarely took Laney on the weekends he was supposed to. So why would he suddenly want an eight-year-old child running around full time? It didn't make any sense."

Fernando didn't say anything for a long moment, waiting for her to continue. It was a technique detectives used with suspects. Interesting how difficult it was to stay silent when you wanted nothing more than to loudly and earnestly proclaim your innocence.

Somehow, she managed to hold her tongue. The forensic van had arrived, Jackie the tech going to work.

"Look, I can help collect evidence—"

"No, you can't." Fernando cut her off midsentence. "You need to give me your gun and your shield and head home."

She stared at him. "Why are you taking my gun and shield?"

"You know why." Fernando held out his hand impatiently. "You're too close to this, and we need to clear you before I can let you come back to work."

Clear her? It took a moment for the realization to sink in. "You can't seriously believe I'm a suspect? Come on,

Loo, I was home all night and worked my shift all day. Besides, I would never do something like this."

Fernando waved his fingers. "Shield and gun."

Feeling as if she'd walked into some sort of horror show, Maggie removed her badge and gun from her belt holster. After dropping them into his outstretched hand, she turned and yanked the driver's door of her SUV open.

Simmons had joined Fernando. No one said a word as she slid in behind the wheel, started the engine, cranked the air conditioning, and backed away from the crime scene.

She drove in a daze, hardly able to comprehend what had just happened. She'd found her ex-husband's dead body lying in the middle of nowhere and was now a suspect in his murder.

The worst part of all? The small wave of relief that washed over her at knowing Laney's custody arrangement wouldn't change. A man had lost his life, had been deliberately shot in the head. It was wrong to be relived.

Yet marrying Tate had been a mistake. One she'd done to cover another lapse in judgment. At the time, she'd thought marrying Tate was the right thing to do, for Laney's sake.

She'd been wrong.

As she drove to her mother's house, she couldn't help but wonder if this was God's way of punishing her for her sins. And while she may deserve God's penance, Laney didn't.

Her daughter was the true innocent in this.

RETIRED former Navy SEAL Dallas Hoffman glanced at his chocolate lab, Romeo, via the rearview mirror. Romeo looked content despite the way the poor canine had been cooped up longer than usual. "We'll be there soon, boy," he said.

Romeo thumped his tail in response.

His sister, Brenda, called him constantly for help. She ran a small tourist store in downtown Fredericksburg, and her latest proposition was that she wanted him to be her private, unpaid security guard to prevent shoplifting. Apparently some of the teenagers thought it was a game to steal stuff they didn't even want, just to prove they could get away with it. Brenda's son, Jason, was one of the perpetrators. Since Brenda's divorce, Jason had been acting out. This was just one of the latest examples.

Dallas loved his sister and cared about his nephew, so he always came when she called. Yet he couldn't help feeling frustrated. Her crisis situations were nothing compared to what he'd dealt with during his twenty-year stint as a Navy SEAL.

He instinctively rubbed his sore left shoulder. The one that had been reconstructed back in January after their last op had gone sideways. He and his five teammates, Mason, Kaleb, Hudd, Dawson, and Nico had been lucky to survive, but Jaydon hadn't. Their extraction had been dicey, tangos shooting hot on their heels as they hit the water to head for the ship waiting for them. They'd never anticipated an underwater bomb.

Until the explosion had sent them spinning and tumbling through the water.

His taking shrapnel in the shoulder and Kaleb Tyson's blown-out knee had been the least damaging of the assault. Senior Chief Mason Gray had lost his hearing in one ear and suffered a partial loss of hearing in the other, Hudd Foster had lost vision in one eye and suffered debilitating headaches, Dawson Steele had taken a belly load of shrapnel that had resulted in four separate surgeries, and Nico Ramirez had ruptured his Achilles tendon. Nico was also Jaydon's swim buddy, and between them, they'd done CPR on him in the water, fighting hard to save Jaydon's life.

To no avail.

Dallas rubbed his aching shoulder again. The doc had told him he'd never have full range of motion, but he hadn't wanted to believe it.

Yet seven months post-surgery, and the reconstructed joint was nowhere near where he'd hoped it would be. He'd thought he'd be able to get back into the life. Not a Navy SEAL, as that was a young man's game, but in some sort of law enforcement.

He'd pretty much figured out retirement wasn't his thing. Responding to his sister's complaints wasn't enough either. He was growing bored, and that wasn't good.

Nico was searching for Jaydon Rampart's younger sister, Ava, who'd been missing for months now. Unfortunately, the trail had gone cold. Nico had followed up a few leads that had gone nowhere. The last time he'd connected with Nico, his teammate had assured him he'd call if he found anything.

Still, driving between Austin and Fredericksburg was getting old. Maybe it was time to head back to San Diego. He keenly missed the ocean.

He instinctively slowed down when he saw several police vehicles off to the side of the highway. Something was going on, they were setting up a tent while buzzards circled overhead. The situation piqued his interest, but he kept going. Brenda was waiting, she wanted him to have another heart-to-heart talk with Jason.

When he came up behind another SUV, he decided to pass. There was no one coming the other way, so he moved over to go around it. But as he drove by, he did a double take when he glimpsed the driver.

Wait a minute, was that Maggie Stevenson? He lightly tapped the horn to get her attention. She turned and scowled at him, until recognition dawned in her eyes.

He smiled and waved, but she didn't return the gesture. Instead, she hit the gas, leaping ahead of him. A car was coming toward him, forcing him to return to his lane, behind Maggie.

Her cold-shoulder reaction bothered him. They'd dated nonstop for three months between deployments. One night they'd gotten carried away, making it the best night of his life, followed by the one he regretted the most. He'd known that he loved her and planned to make things right, but he had urgently been called out to another deployment. That was how it happened sometimes with the SEAL teams. He'd promised Maggie he'd call when he was back stateside, but unfortunately, that hadn't happened for almost six months. When he'd finally gotten back on US soil, he'd called only to find out she was Maggie Chandler now because she'd recently gotten married.

Married. Despite what he'd thought they'd shared.

Fast forward nine years to now. She was the one who'd found someone else while he'd been gone, so why had she looked so angry with him? Irritated, he followed her all the way into town.

To a small ranch house located on the other side of the city from where his sister lived.

He drove slowly past her house, wondering if he should get out and approach, when she got out of the car, slammed the door, and stalked down the driveway to the street. He hit the brake, stopping the car.

Maggie marched up to the vehicle, glaring at him as he

lowered the window. "What are you doing? Why are you following me?"

"Nice to see y'all too, Mags."

Her brown eyes flashed with anger. "Don't call me that. Just tell me what you're doing here?"

Romeo let out a whine as if he didn't understand why she was yelling at him. Frankly, Dallas couldn't quite figure out what had gotten her so riled up either. "Easy, Romeo, it's okay."

For the first time, Maggie seemed to notice the dog. Her features relaxed just a bit, before her gaze turned back to him. "Well?"

"If you must know, I'm heading to my sister's place. When I saw you on the highway, I thought it would be nice to stop and say hey."

She narrowed her gaze. "After nine years of being who knows where, you just decided to follow me? To say hello? Do you think I'm stupid? I'm not buying your act."

"It's not an act." Dallas wasn't the type to get mad easily, but he felt his temper start to slip. "You don't want to talk, fine. I wasn't trying to follow or stalk you. I was just being neighborly."

"Neighborly?" Her face paled to the point he feared she might fall over. "You *live* here now?"

She looked appalled at the possibility. He couldn't figure out why she was acting so strangely. He was the one who'd been heartbroken. She was the one who'd moved on to someone else. He instinctively looked at her left hand, she wasn't wearing a wedding ring. Which didn't mean much.

"Dallas, are you living here in Fredericksburg?" she asked again.

"Not exactly, but lately I've been in town more often

than not. I've been helping my sister, Brenda. She's having some trouble with her son, Jason."

"Yes, I know Brenda and Jason, that's nice of you to help them out." She took a step back and forced a smile. To his eye, it looked more like a grimace. Suddenly she seemed nicer. "Well, it was great to catch up with you, Dallas. I'm sorry you caught me at a bad time, I—uh, need to get inside."

Before he could offer to meet her at a time that was more convenient, the front door of the small ranch house banged open, and a young girl came running outside. She wore a pink shirt, worn jean shorts, and flip-flops in deference to the heat. She had long blond hair, pulled back into a ponytail the same color and style as Maggie's. Which made sense when the girl shouted, "Mom! Nanna says to hurry up. Your spaghetti is getting cold!"

"Coming, Laney." The fake smile seemed frozen in place. "I really have to go. Bye, Dallas." She lightly ran toward her daughter, urging the girl toward the house.

"Who was that man, Mom?" he heard Laney ask. "Did you have to arrest him or something?"

"Oh, no, he's not a criminal. Just an old friend." Maggie opened the front door and nearly pushed the girl inside. Then she turned to look back at him for a long moment before she followed Laney inside, the door banging shut behind her.

Romeo let out a short bark as if asking what on earth was taking so long.

"Okay, boy. I hear you." He rolled up the window and put the car in gear. It seemed Maggie may have some role within the police department, considering her daughter's question about arresting him.

Had she come from the police scene he'd passed along

the way? It seemed likely. He hadn't seen a badge or gun, so maybe she had some other role. Or she was off duty.

Yet as he drove through town to get to his sister's house, he couldn't help but wonder if he'd really seen a flash of fear and apprehension in Maggie's dark brown eyes.

And if so, why?

Made in the USA
Columbia, SC
19 April 2024